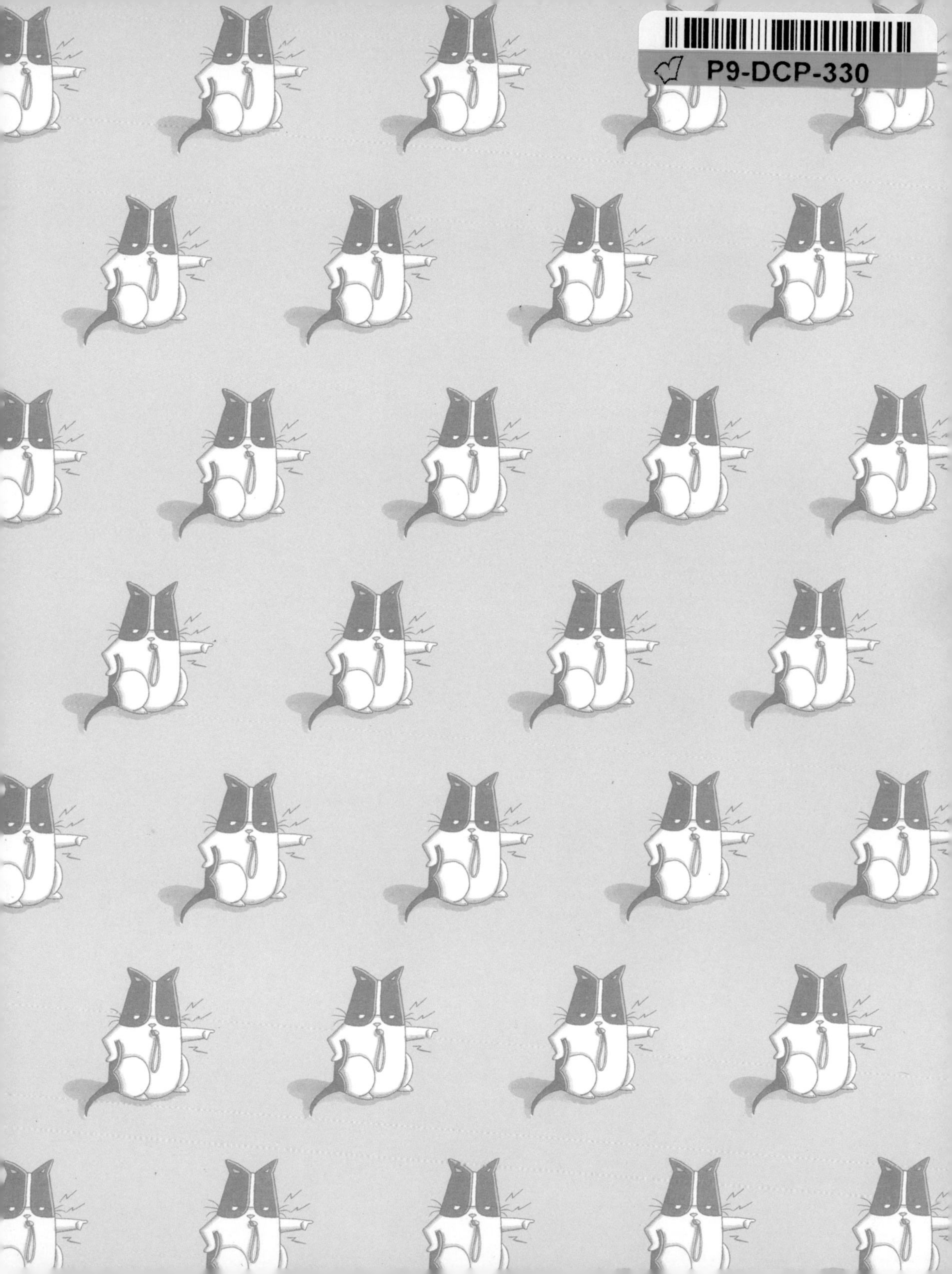

BINKY

TAKES CHARGE

KIDS CAN PRESS

For Meggy, Ethan, their kitties and the puppy I hope they get some day

Text and illustrations © 2012 Ashley Spires

All rights reserved. No part of this publication may be reproduced, stored in a retrieval system or transmitted, in any form or by any means, without the prior written permission of Kids Can Press Ltd. or, in case of photocopying or other reprographic copying, a license from The Canadian Copyright Licensing Agency (Access Copyright). For an Access Copyright license, visit www.accesscopyright.ca or call toll free to 1-800-893-5777.

Kids Can Press acknowledges the financial support of the Government of Ontario, through the Ontario Media Development Corporation's Ontario Book Initiative; the Ontario Arts Council; the Canada Council for the Arts; and the Government of Canada, through the BPIDP, for our publishing activity.

Published in Canada by
Kids Can Press Ltd.
25 Dockside Drive
Toronto, ON M5A 0B5

Published in the U.S. by
Kids Can Press Ltd.
2250 Military Road
Tonawanda, NY 14150

www.kidscanpress.com

The artwork in this book was rendered in ink, watercolor, cat fur, bits of kitty litter, the occasional paw print and dog slobber.
The text is set in Fontoon.

Edited by Tara Walker and Karen Li
Series designer: Karen Powers
Designed by Rachel Di Salle

The hardcover edition of this book is smyth sewn casebound.
The paperback edition of this book is limp sewn with a drawn-on cover.
Manufactured in Shen Zhen, Guang Dong, P.R. China, in 4/2012 by Printplus Limited.

CM 12 0 9 8 7 6 5 4 3 2 1
CM PA 12 0 9 8 7 6 5 4 3 2 1

Library and Archives Canada Cataloguing in Publication

Spires, Ashley, 1978–
     Binky takes charge / by Ashley Spires.

(A Binky adventure)
ISBN 978-1-55453-703-7 (bound)   ISBN 978-1-55453-768-6 (pbk.)

     I. Title. II. Series: Spire, Ashley, 1978– . Binky adventure.

PS8637.P57B552 2012   jC813'.6   C2012-900815-X

Kids Can Press is a *lorus*™ Entertainment company

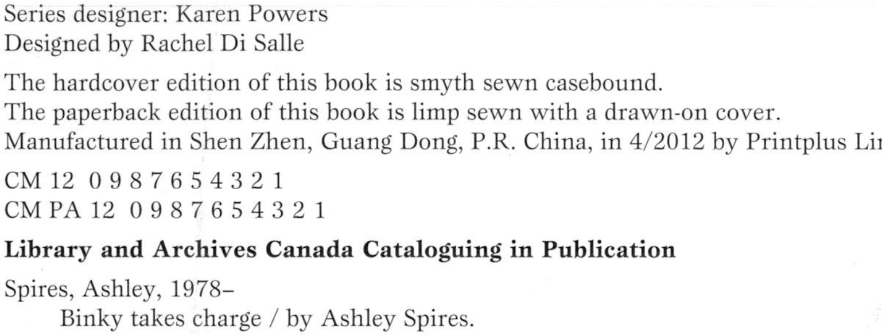

NO CARPETS WERE PEED ON IN THE MAKING OF THIS BOOK. THERE WAS A HAIRBALL ON THE STAIRS, A SERIOUS CASE OF KITTY-LITTER FOOT AND ONE MYSTERIOUS POO NUGGET IN THE BEDROOM, BUT ALL RUGS REMAINED DRY AND URINE-FREE.

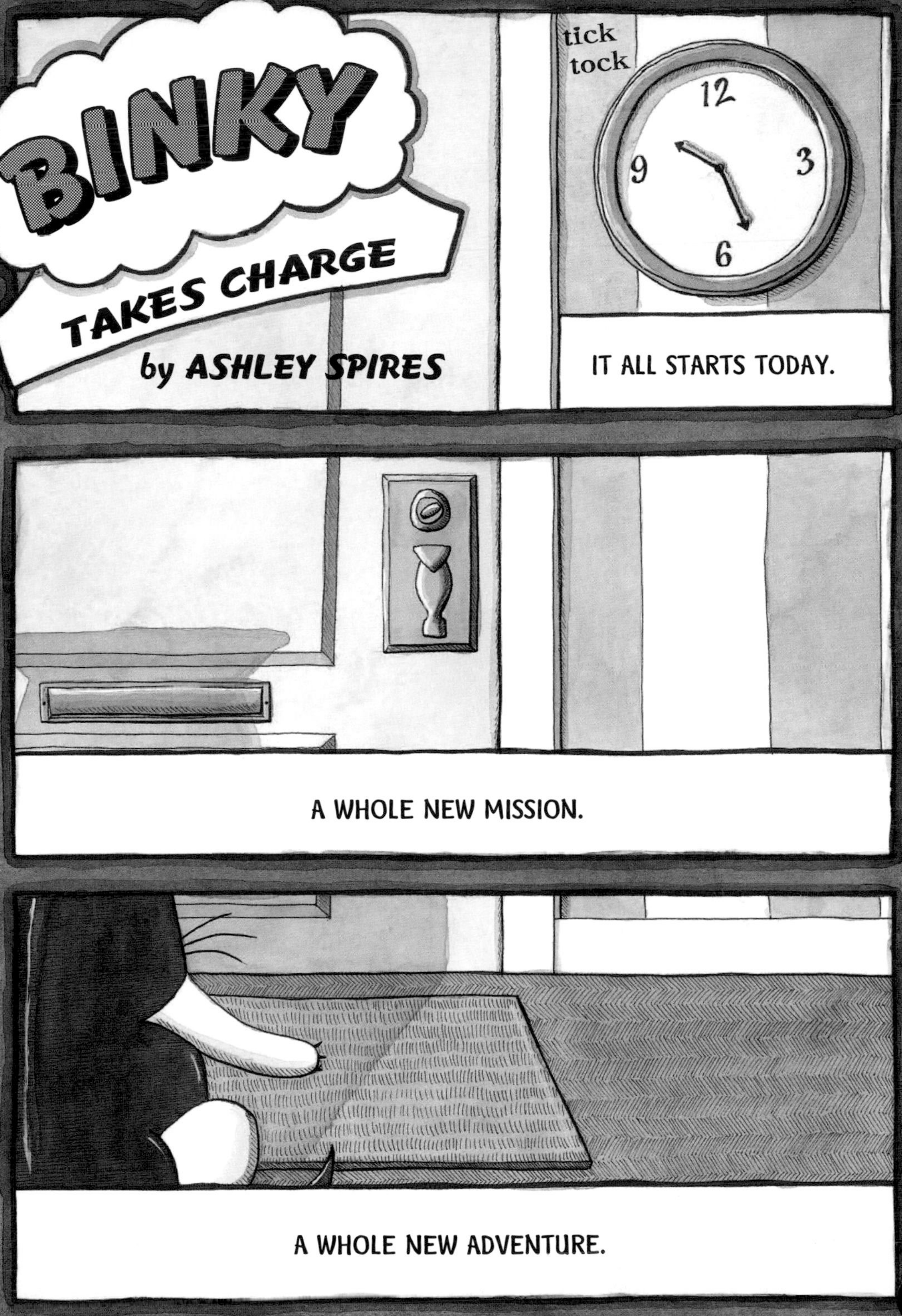
BINKY
TAKES CHARGE
by ASHLEY SPIRES
tick
tock
12
3
6
9
IT ALL STARTS TODAY.
A WHOLE NEW MISSION.
A WHOLE NEW ADVENTURE.

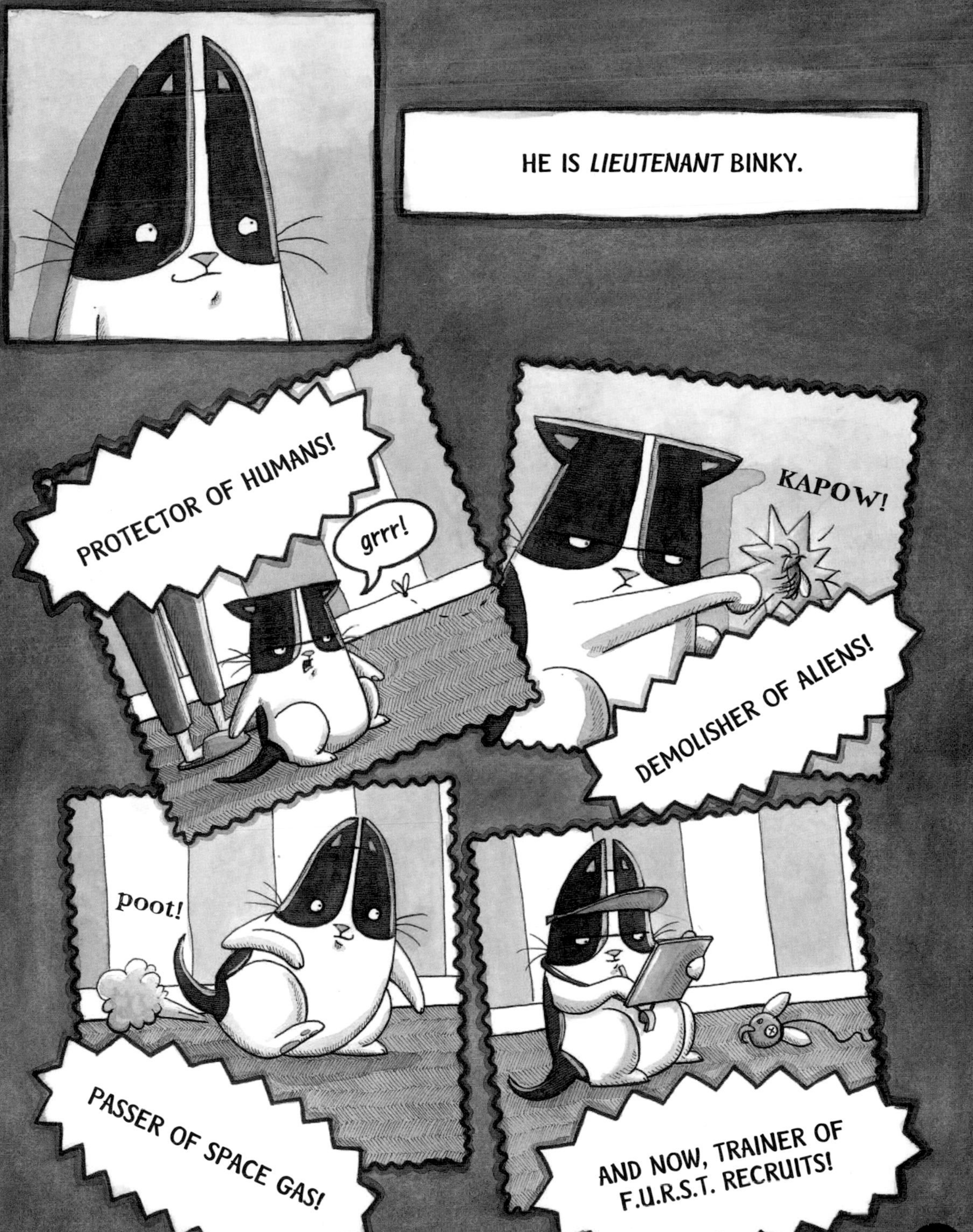
HE IS *LIEUTENANT* BINKY.
PROTECTOR OF HUMANS!
grrr!
KAPOW!
DEMOLISHER OF ALIENS!
poot!
PASSER OF SPACE GAS!
AND NOW, TRAINER OF F.U.R.S.T. RECRUITS!

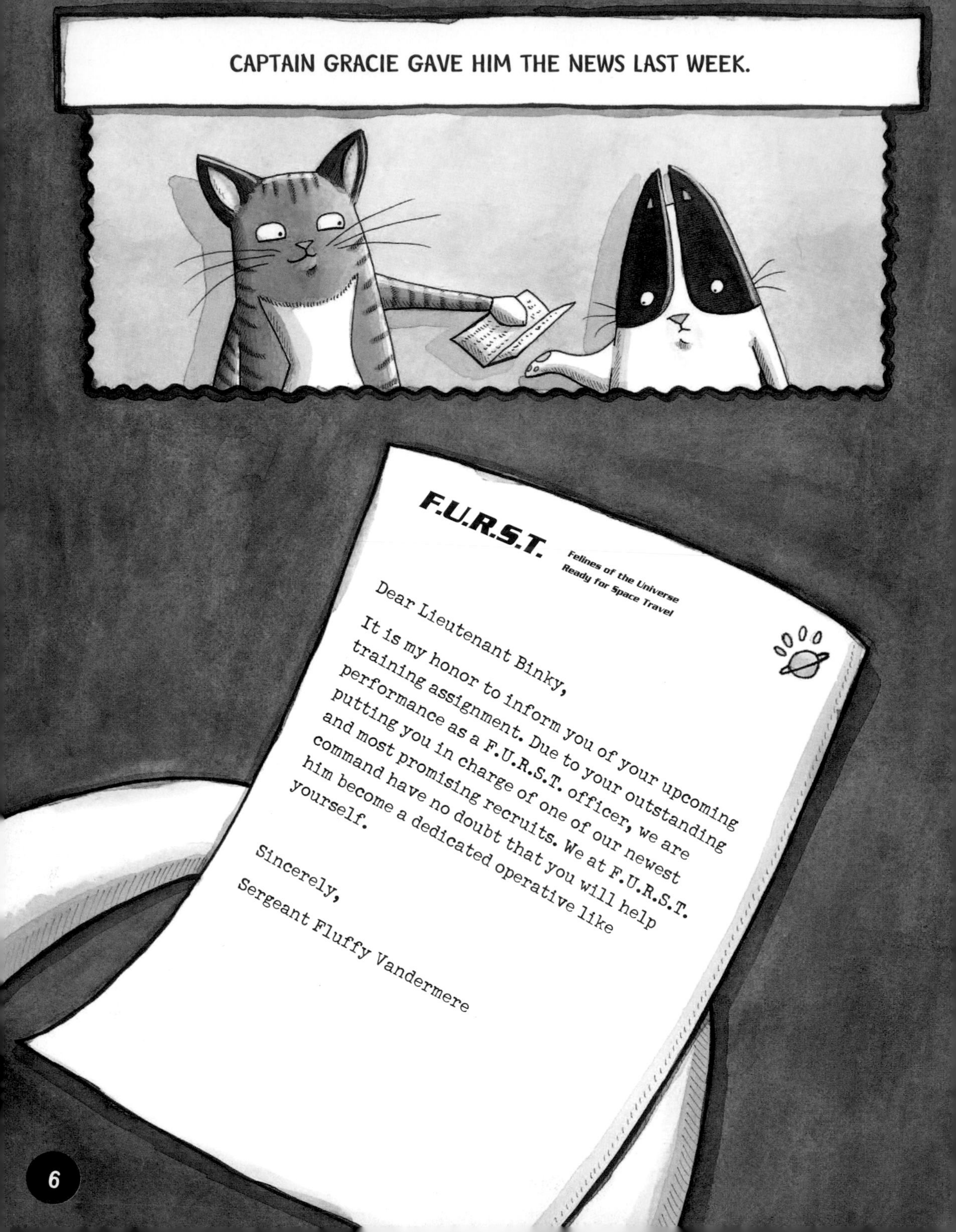
CAPTAIN GRACIE GAVE HIM THE NEWS LAST WEEK.
F.U.R.S.T.
Felines of the Universe Ready for Space Travel
Dear Lieutenant Binky,
It is my honor to inform you of your upcoming training assignment. Due to your outstanding performance as a F.U.R.S.T. officer, we are putting you in charge of one of our newest and most promising recruits. We at F.U.R.S.T. command have no doubt that you will help him become a dedicated operative like yourself.
Sincerely,
Sergeant Fluffy Vandermere

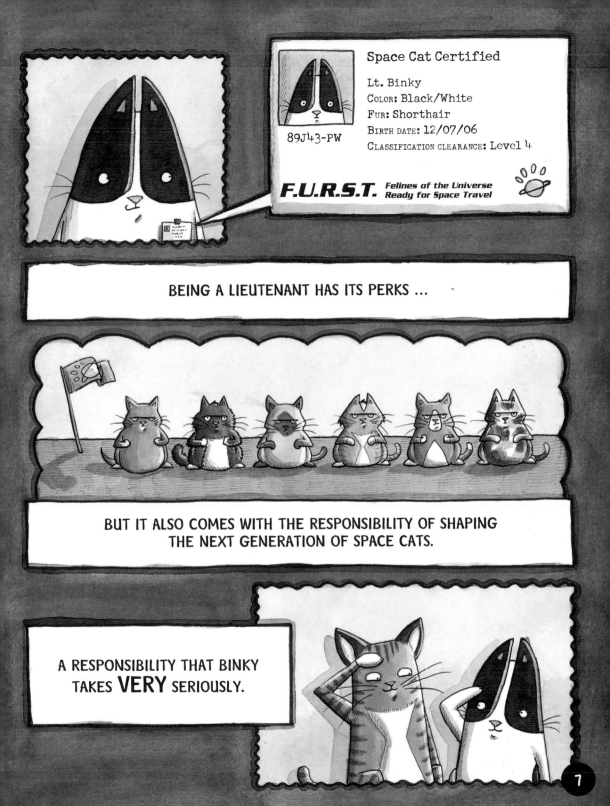

Space Cat Certified

Lt. Binky
COLOR: Black/White
FUR: Shorthair
BIRTH DATE: 12/07/06
CLASSIFICATION CLEARANCE: Level 4

89J43-PW

F.U.R.S.T. Felines of the Universe
Ready for Space Travel

BEING A LIEUTENANT HAS ITS PERKS ...

BUT IT ALSO COMES WITH THE RESPONSIBILITY OF SHAPING
THE NEXT GENERATION OF SPACE CATS.

A RESPONSIBILITY THAT BINKY
TAKES **VERY** SERIOUSLY.

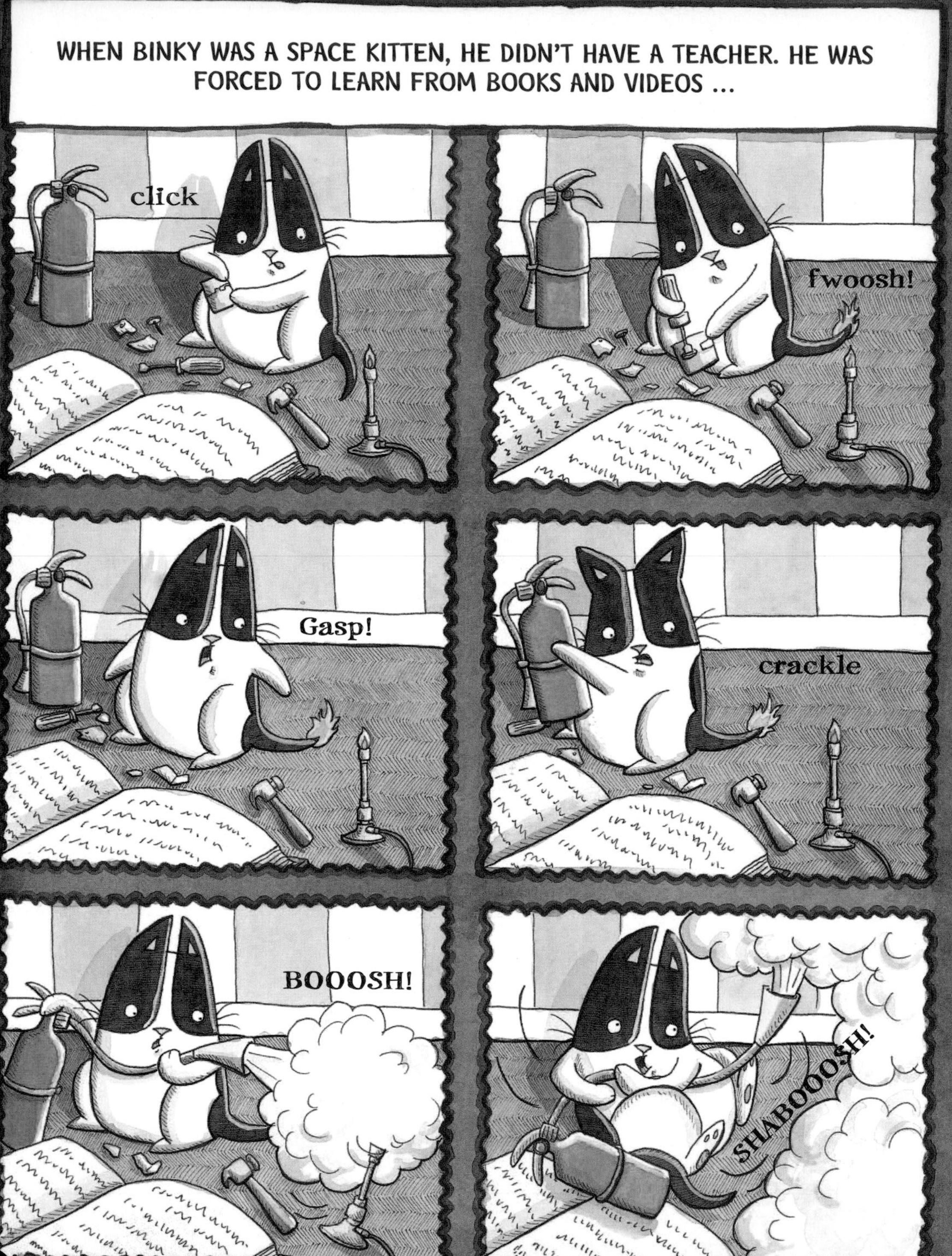
WHEN BINKY WAS A SPACE KITTEN, HE DIDN'T HAVE A TEACHER. HE WAS FORCED TO LEARN FROM BOOKS AND VIDEOS ...
click
fwoosh!
Gasp!
crackle
BOOOSH!
SHABOOOSH!

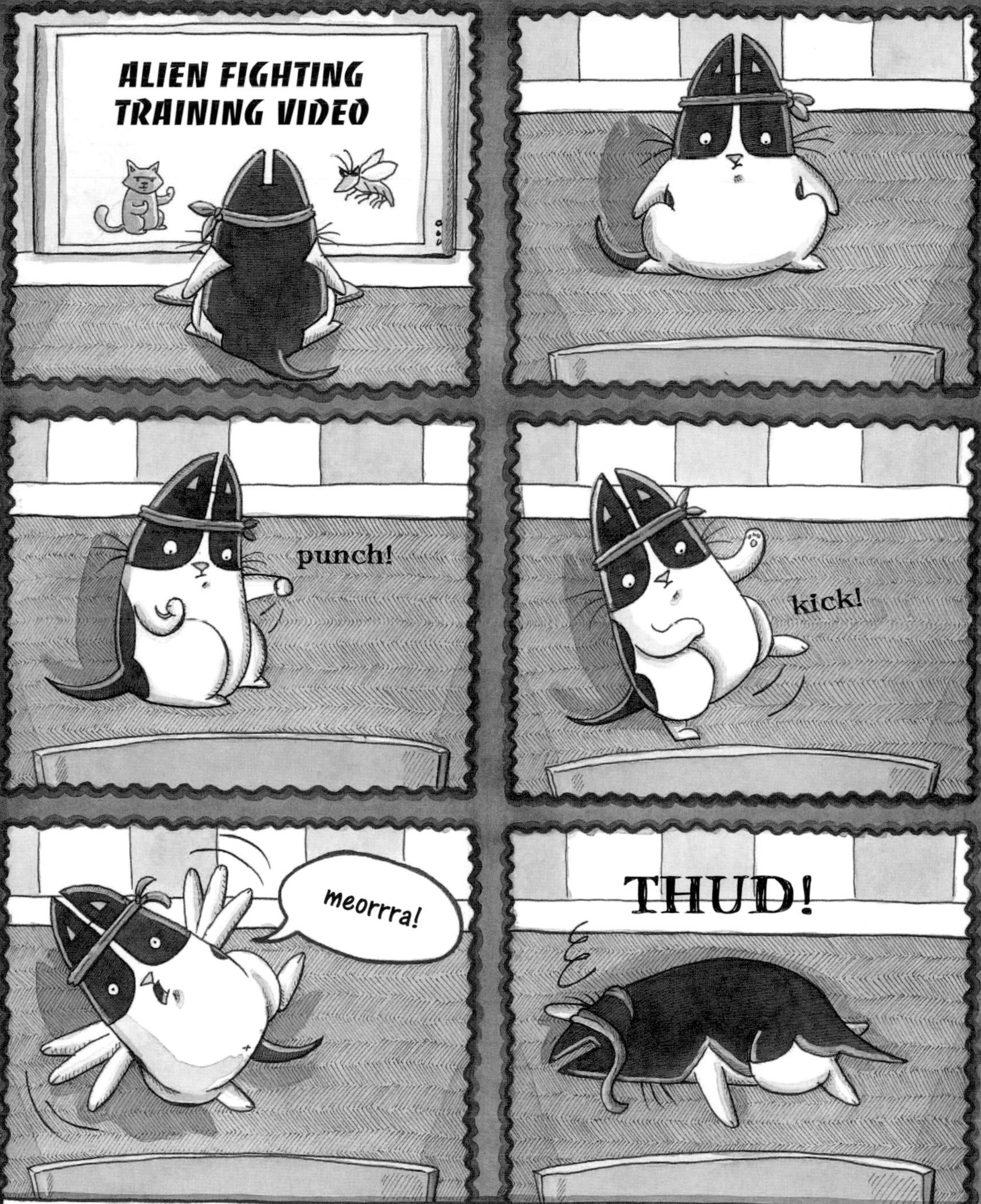
ALIEN FIGHTING
TRAINING VIDEO
punch!
kick!
meorrra!
THUD!

WHICH TURNED OUT TO BE A BIT CHALLENGING.

NOW F.U.R.S.T. ASSIGNS SPACE CADETS TO
LEARN FROM EXPERIENCED OFFICERS.

GRACIE HAS TRAINED MANY SPACE KITTENS.

AND WITH HER HELP, BINKY HAS SPENT THE LAST WEEK
DEVELOPING A COMPLETE SPACE CAT TRAINING PLAN.

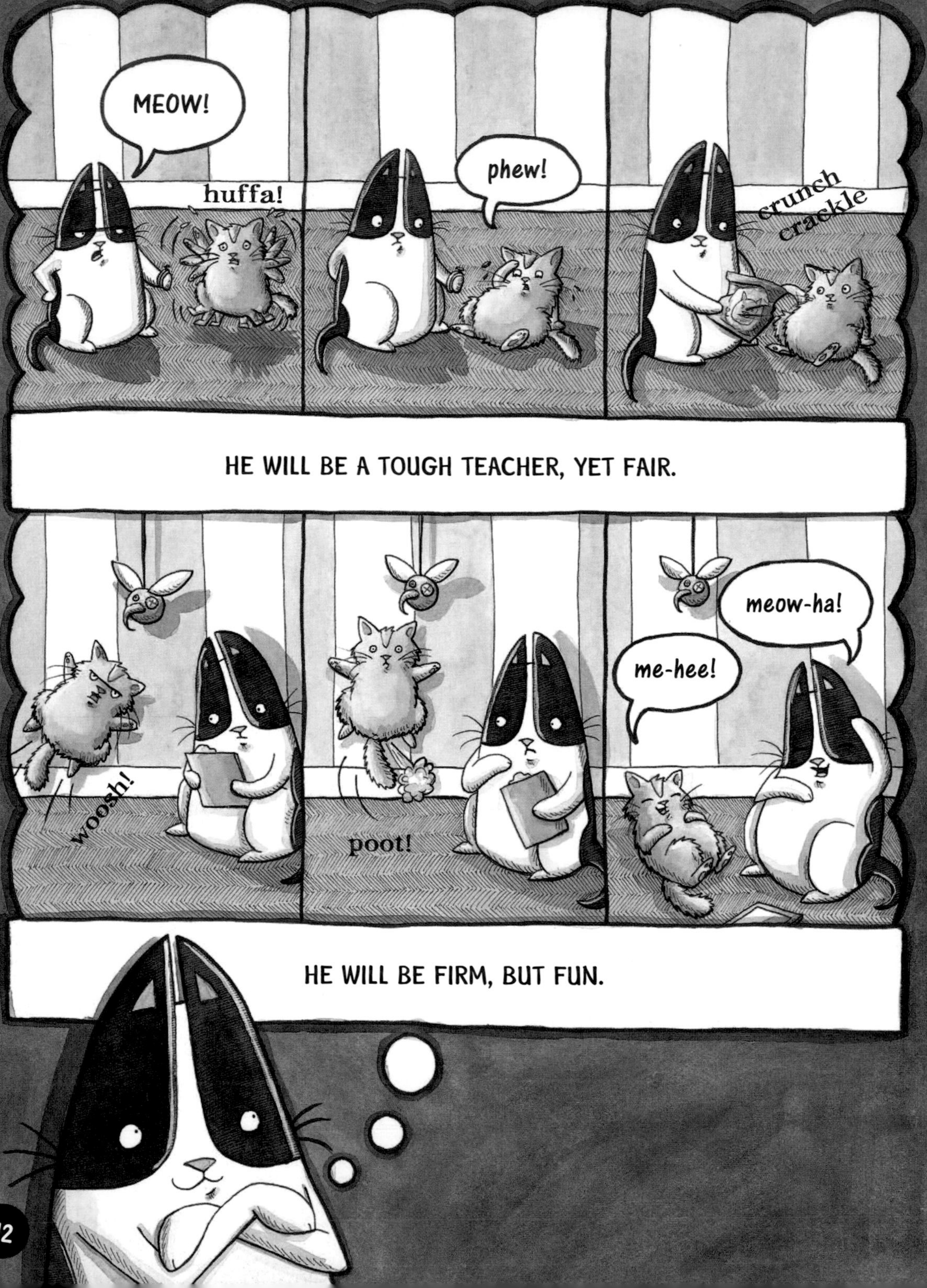
MEOW!
huffa!
phew!
crunch
crackle
HE WILL BE A TOUGH TEACHER, YET FAIR.
woosh!
poot!
me-hee!
meow-ha!
HE WILL BE FIRM, BUT FUN.

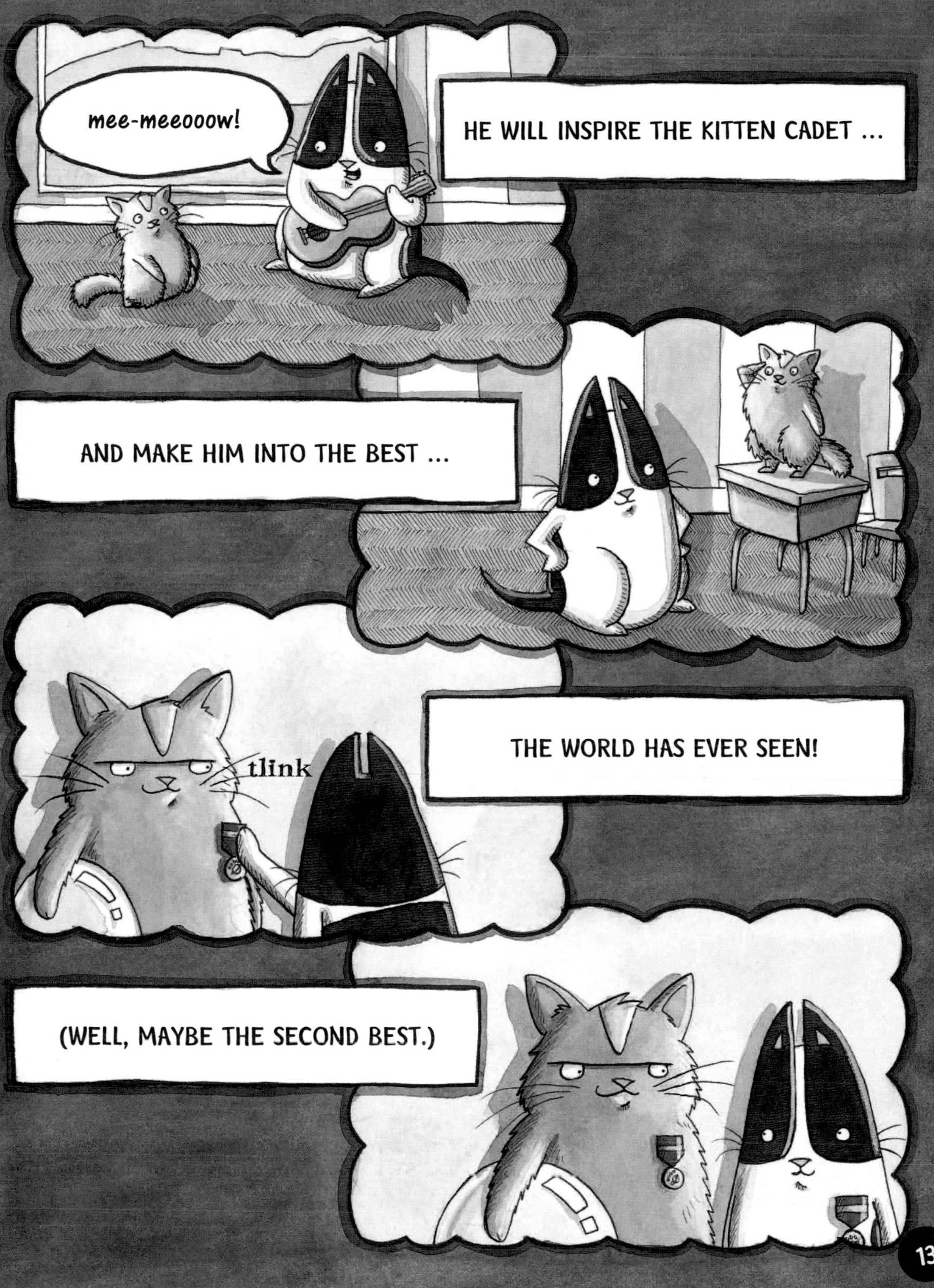
mee-meeooow!
HE WILL INSPIRE THE KITTEN CADET ...
AND MAKE HIM INTO THE BEST ...
tlink
THE WORLD HAS EVER SEEN!
(WELL, MAYBE THE SECOND BEST.)

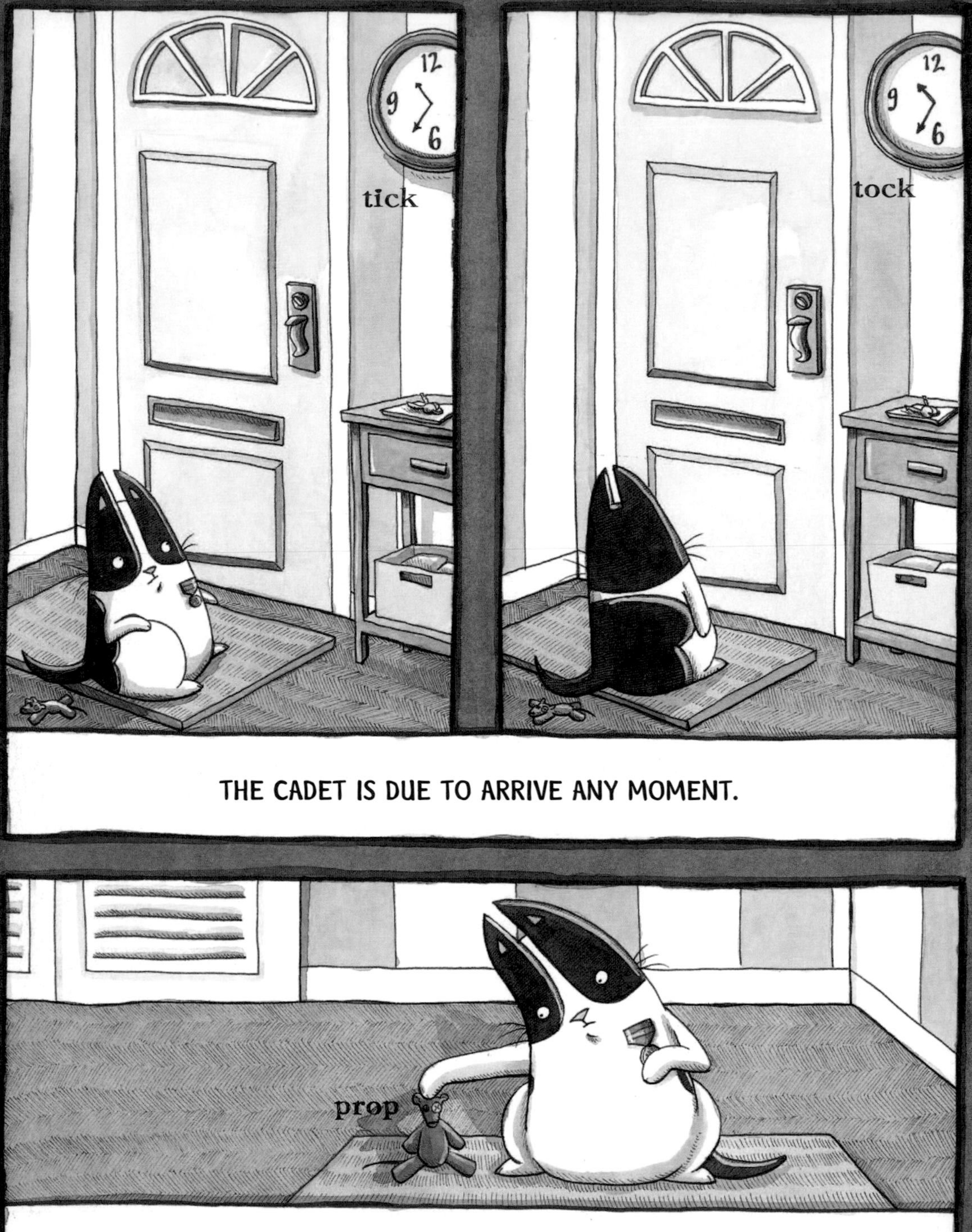
tick
tock
THE CADET IS DUE TO ARRIVE ANY MOMENT.
prop
THIS IS AN IMPORTANT DAY FOR BINKY.

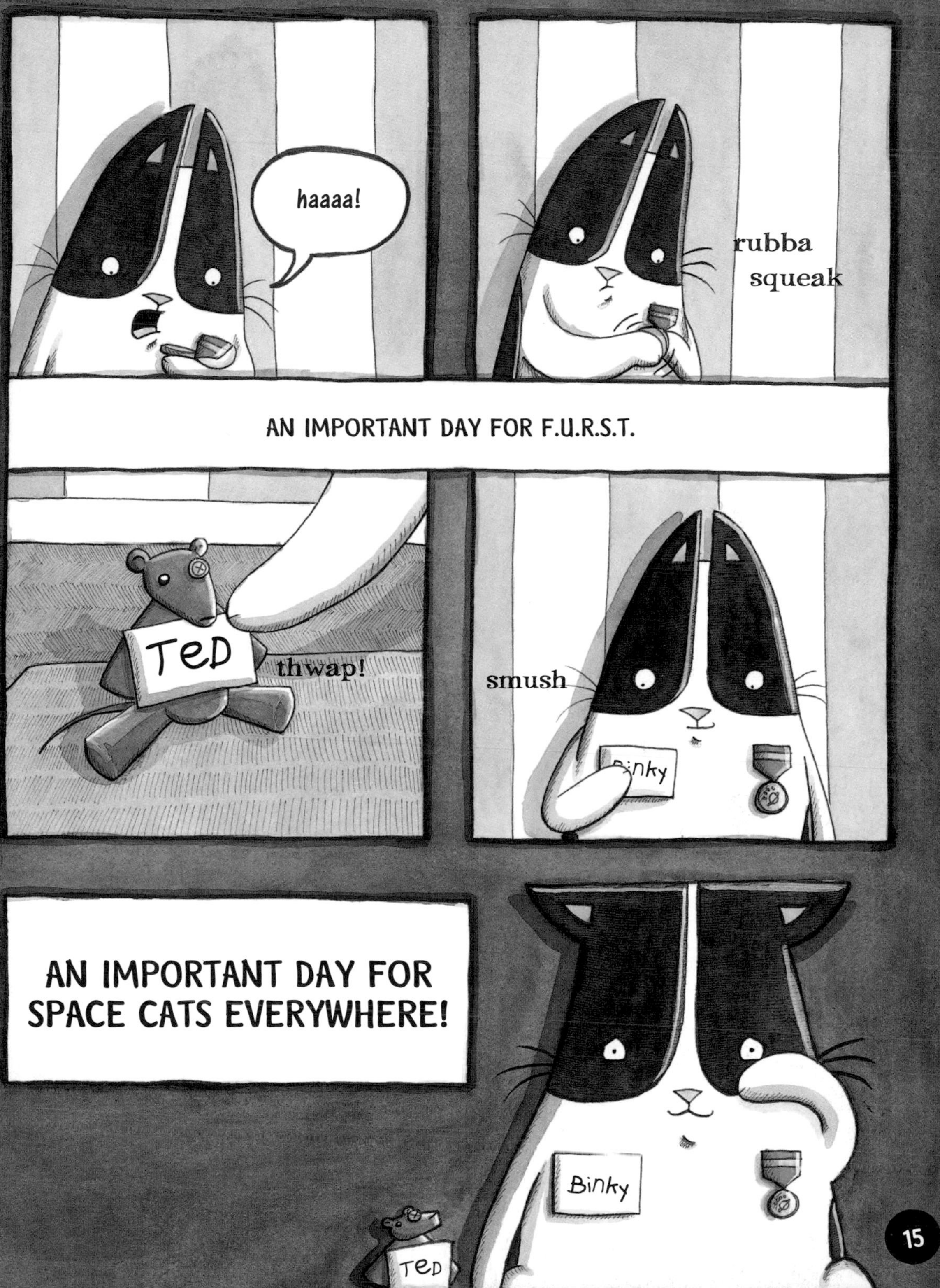
haaaa!
rubba squeak
AN IMPORTANT DAY FOR F.U.R.S.T.
TED
thwap!
smush
Binky
AN IMPORTANT DAY FOR SPACE CATS EVERYWHERE!
Binky
TED

DING!
DONG!
Binky
HE'S HERE!
Oh, he's so cute!
Look how fuzzy he is!
He's so small!

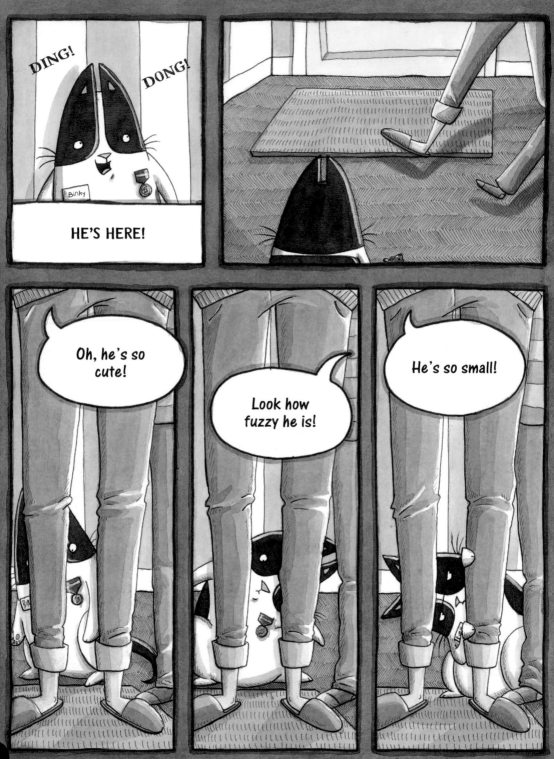

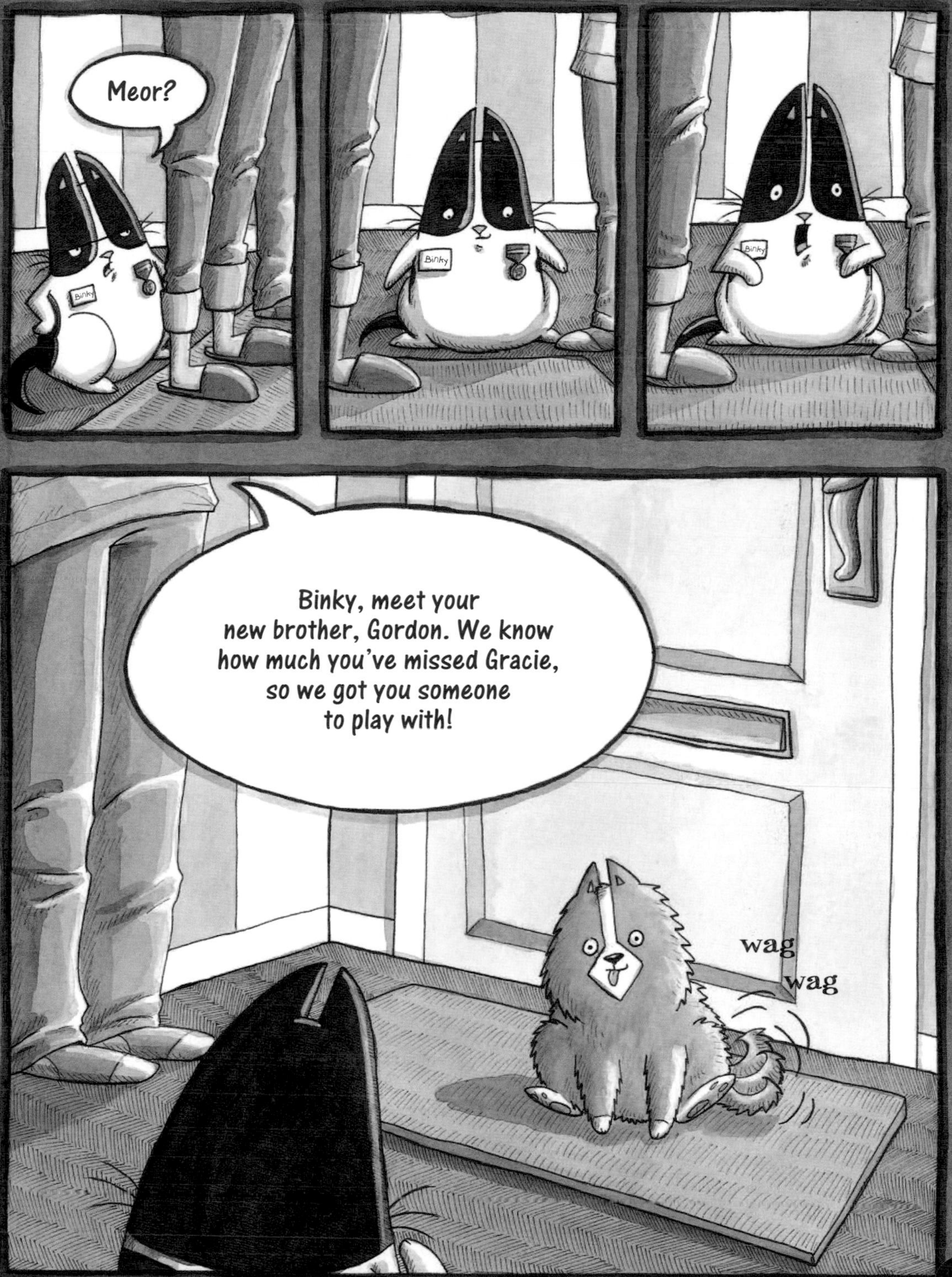
Meor?
Binky
Binky
Binky
Binky, meet your new brother, Gordon. We know how much you've missed Gracie, so we got you someone to play with!
wag
wag

SOMEONE HAS MADE A SERIOUS MISTAKE.

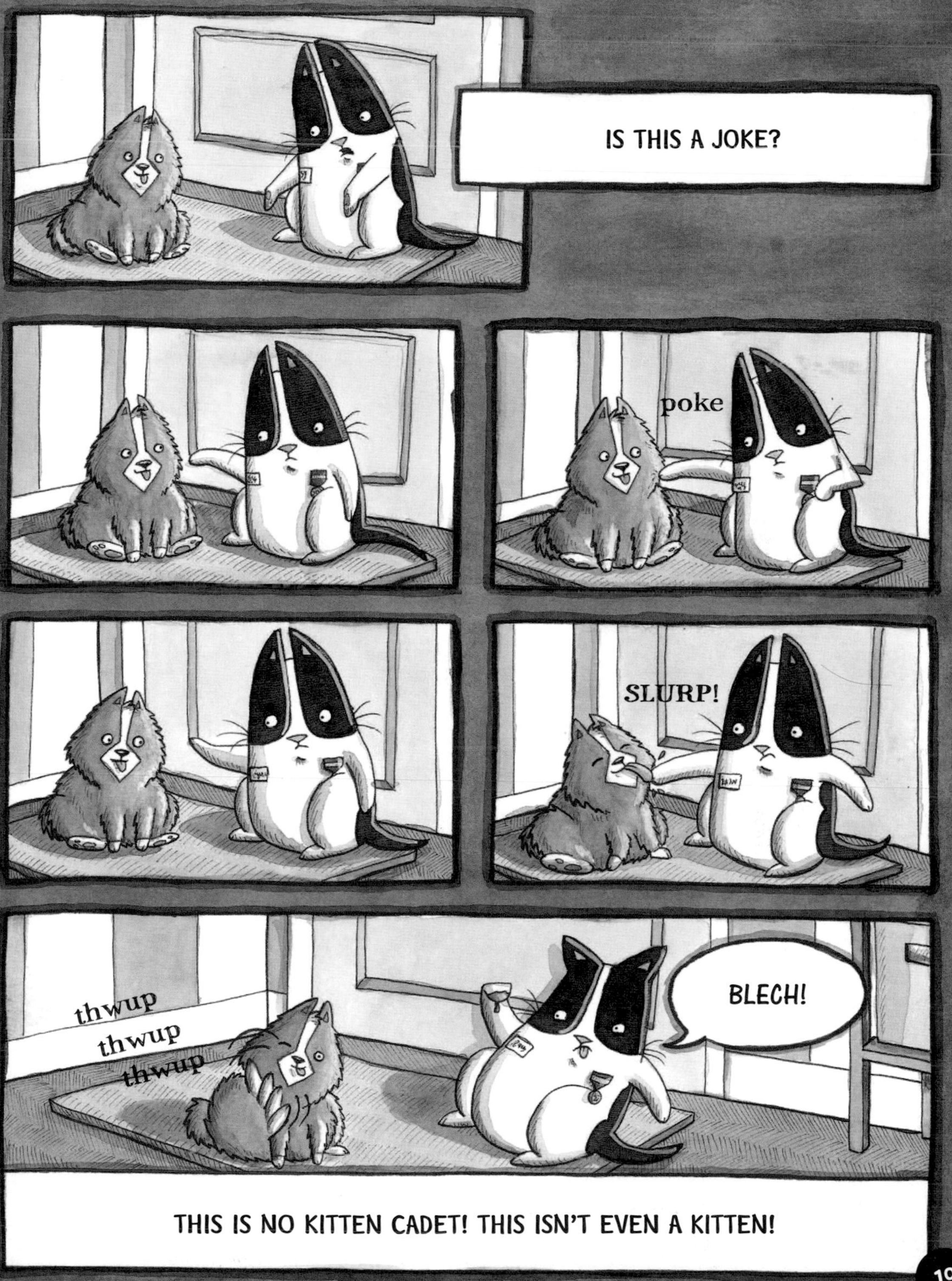
IS THIS A JOKE?
poke
SLURP!
thwup
thwup
thwup
BLECH!
THIS IS NO KITTEN CADET! THIS ISN'T EVEN A KITTEN!

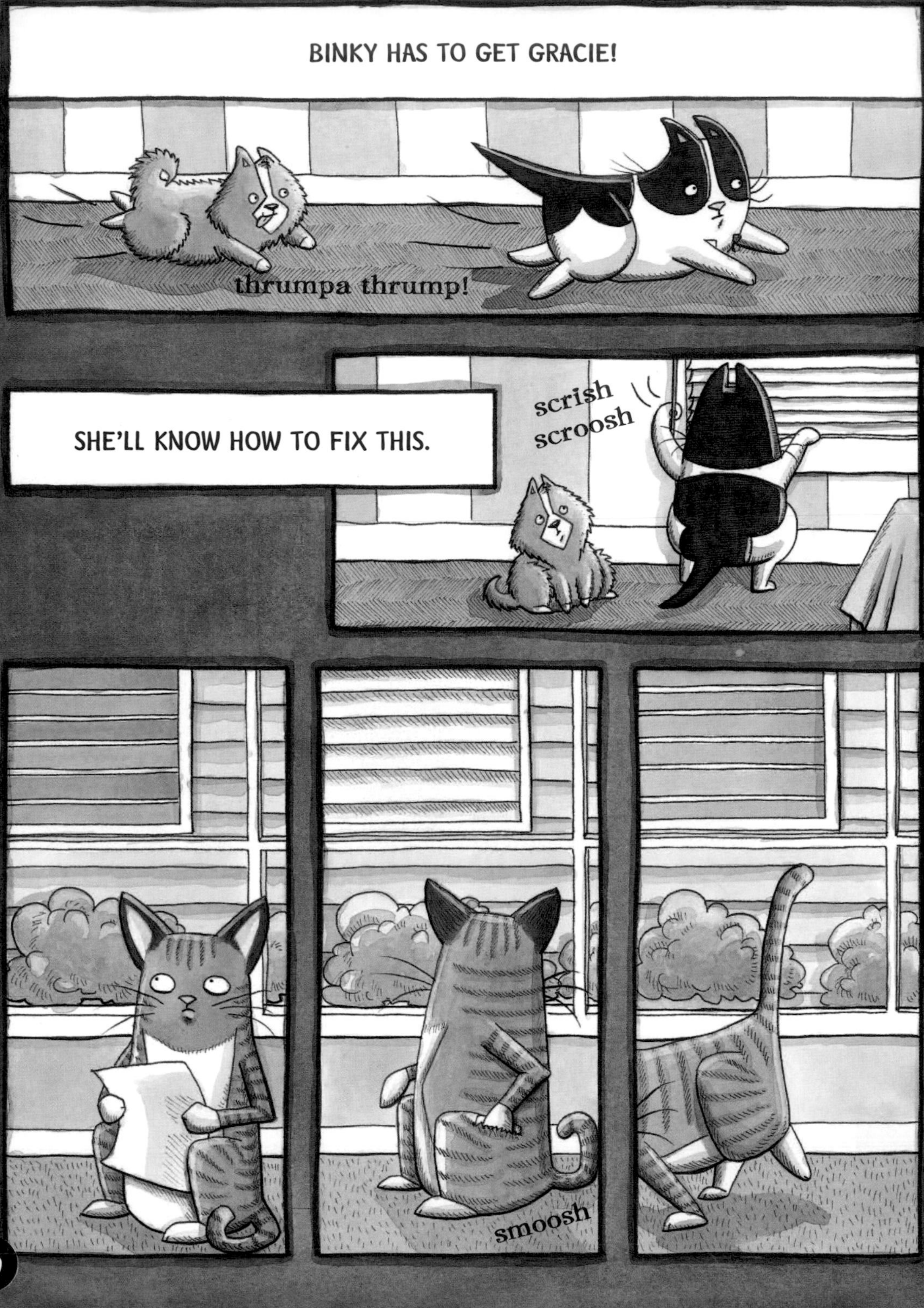
BINKY HAS TO GET GRACIE!
thrumpa thrump!
SHE'LL KNOW HOW TO FIX THIS.
scrish
scroosh
smoosh

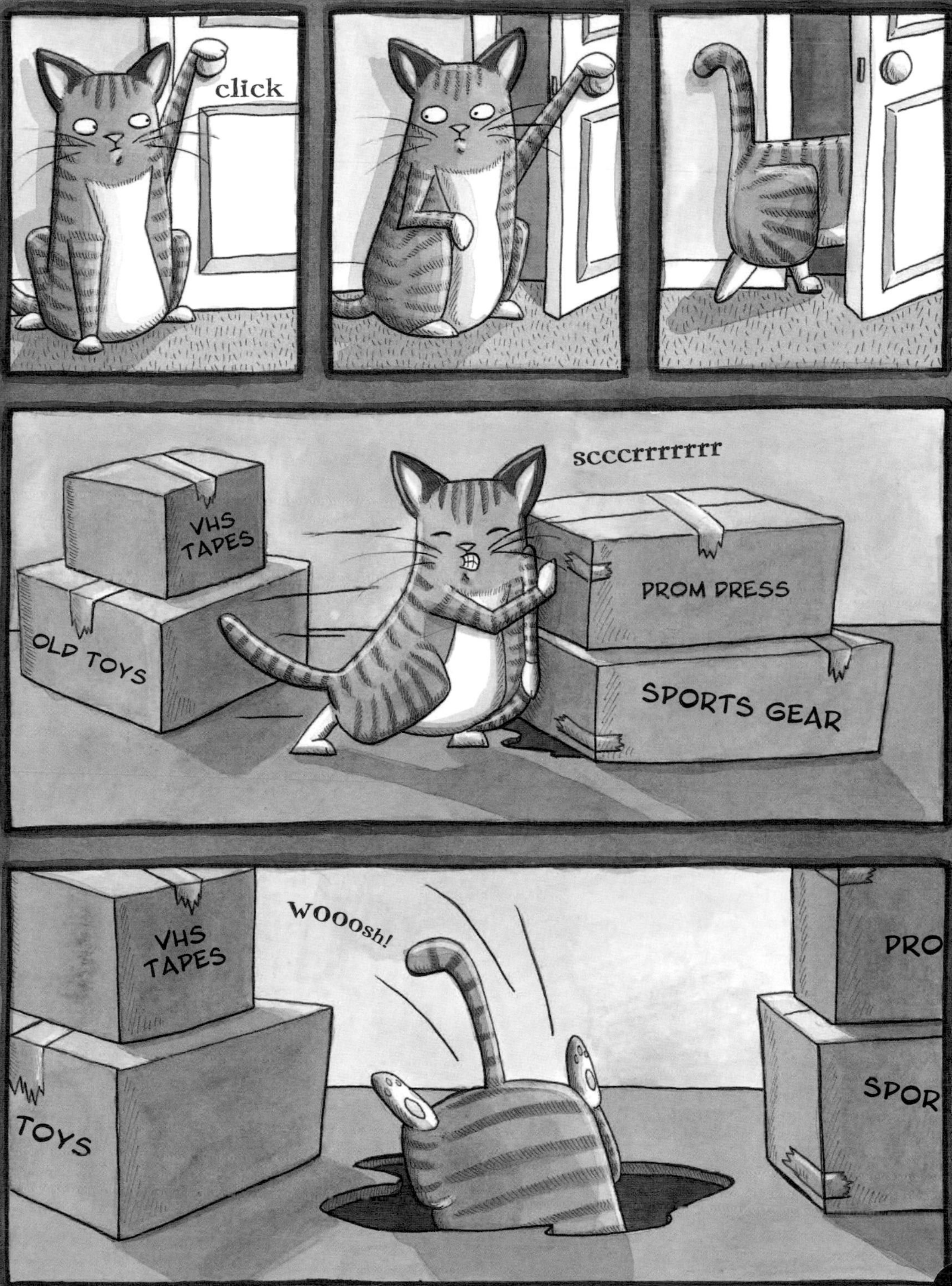
click
scccrrrrrrr
VHS TAPES
OLD TOYS
PROM DRESS
SPORTS GEAR
VHS TAPES
TOYS
WOOOsh!
PRO
SPOR

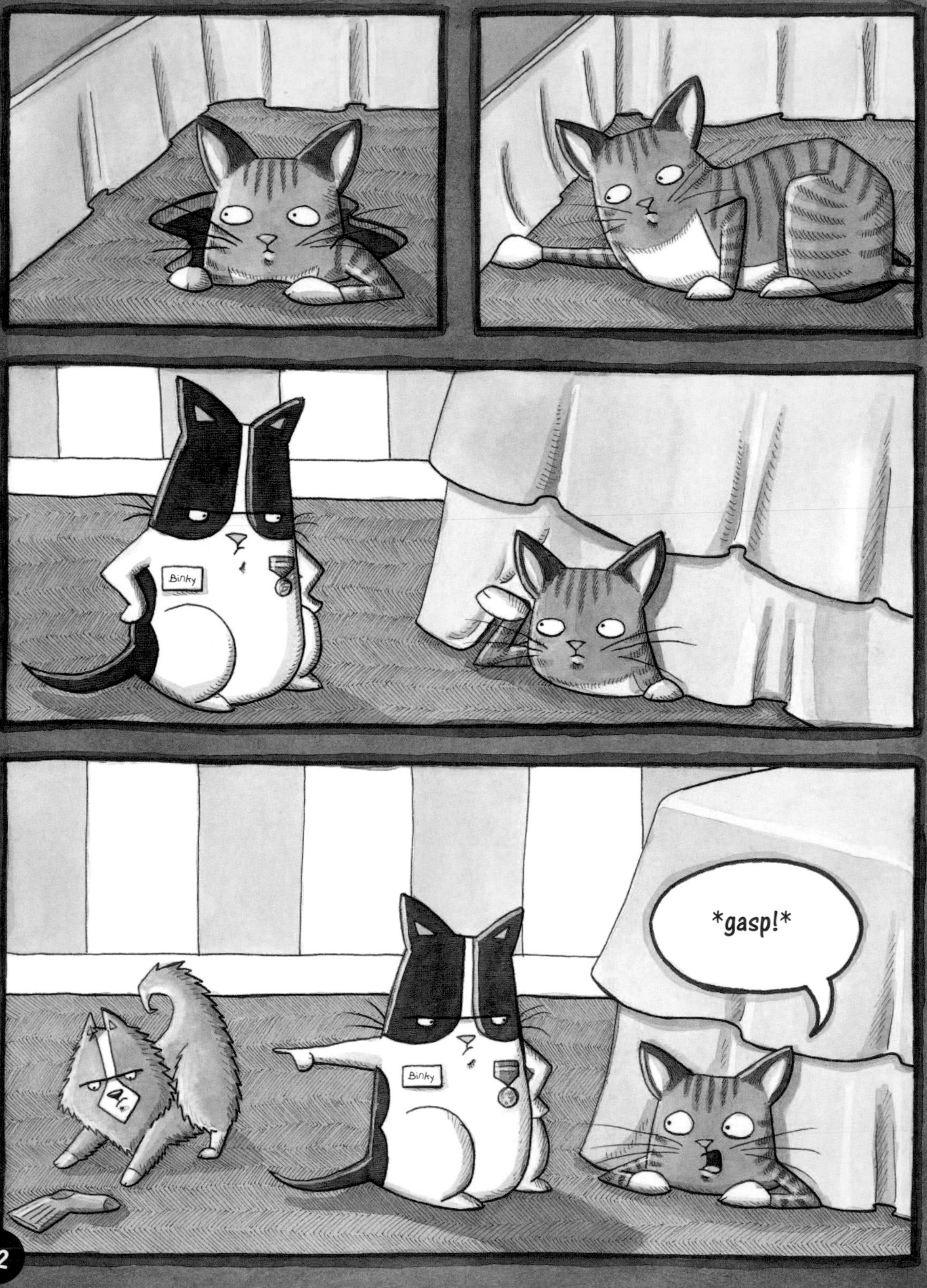
Binky
Binky
gasp!

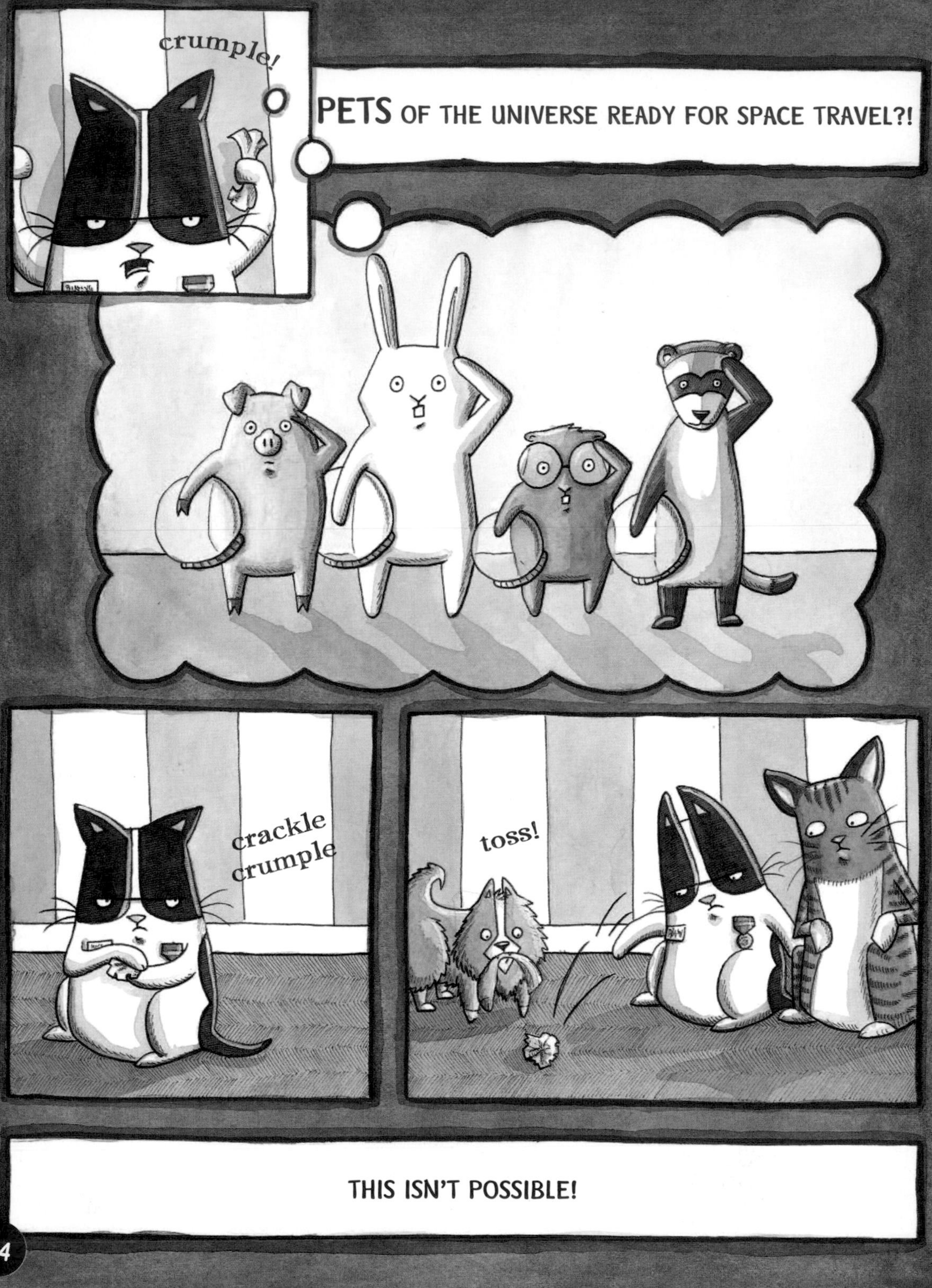
crumple!
PETS OF THE UNIVERSE READY FOR SPACE TRAVEL?!
crackle
crumple
toss!
THIS ISN'T POSSIBLE!

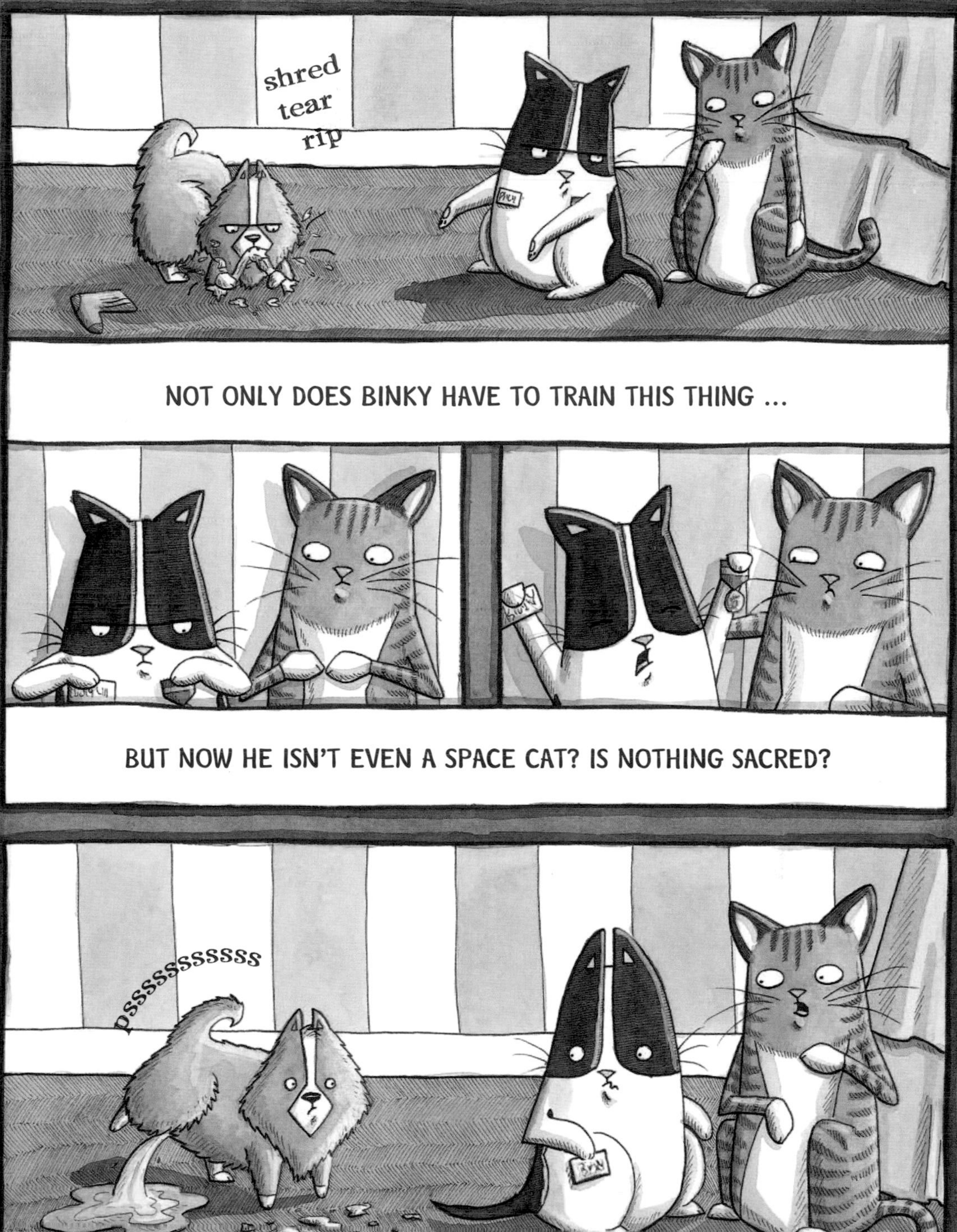
shred
tear
rip
NOT ONLY DOES BINKY HAVE TO TRAIN THIS THING ...
BUT NOW HE ISN'T EVEN A SPACE CAT? IS NOTHING SACRED?
pssssssssssss

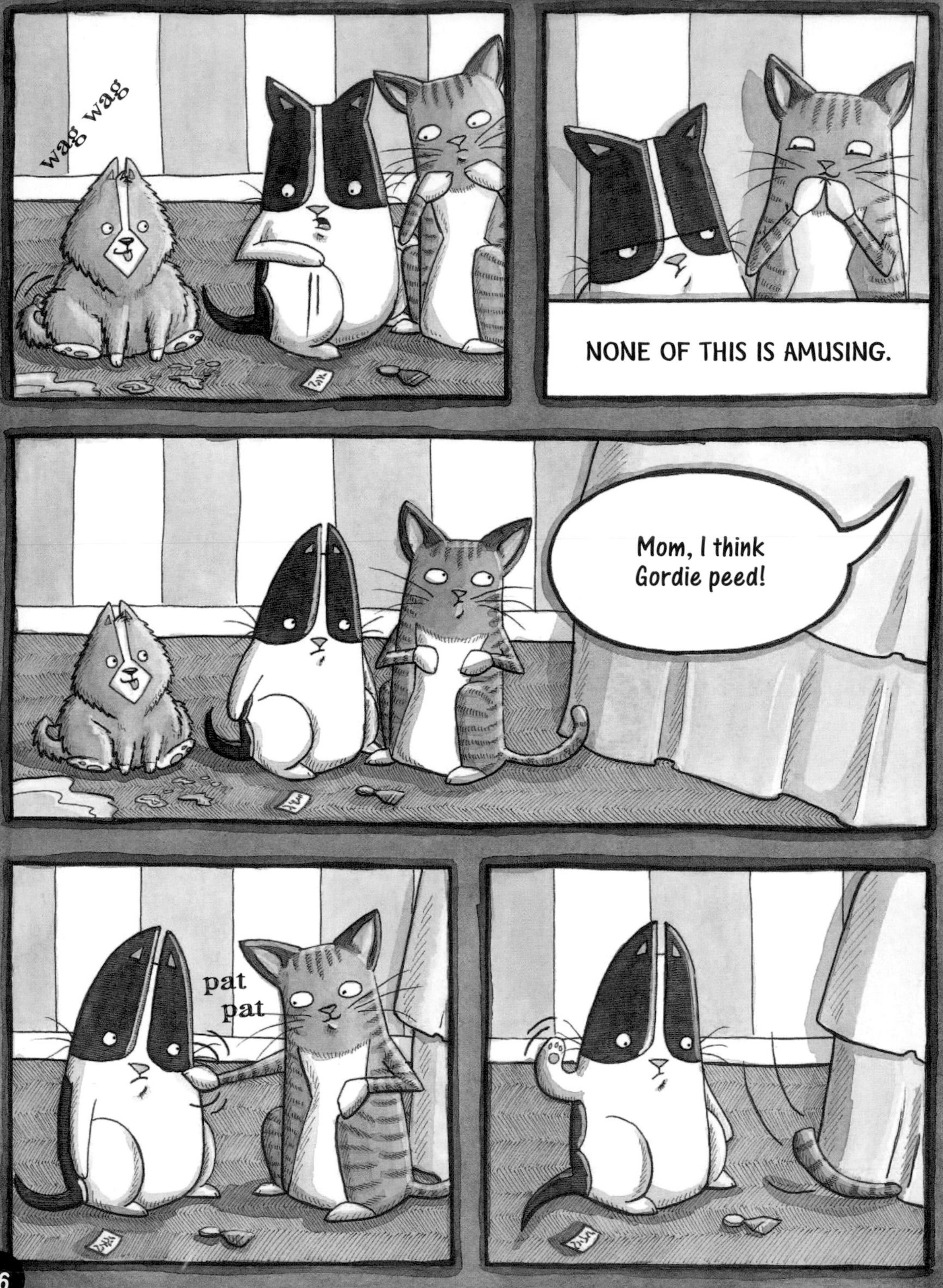
wag wag
NONE OF THIS IS AMUSING.
Mom, I think Gordie peed!
pat pat

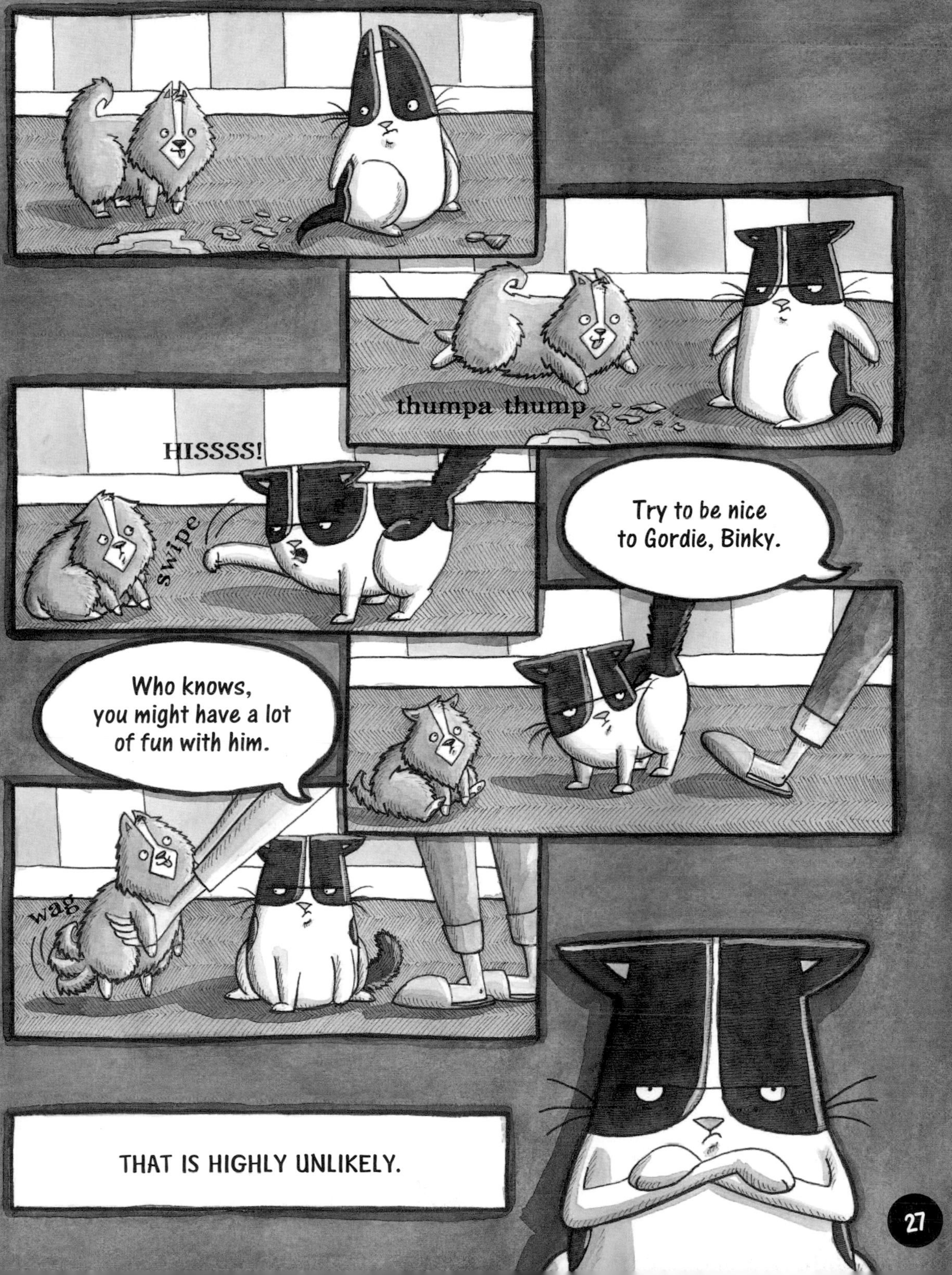

thumpa thump
HISSSS!
swipe
Try to be nice to Gordie, Binky.
Who knows, you might have a lot of fun with him.
wag
THAT IS HIGHLY UNLIKELY.

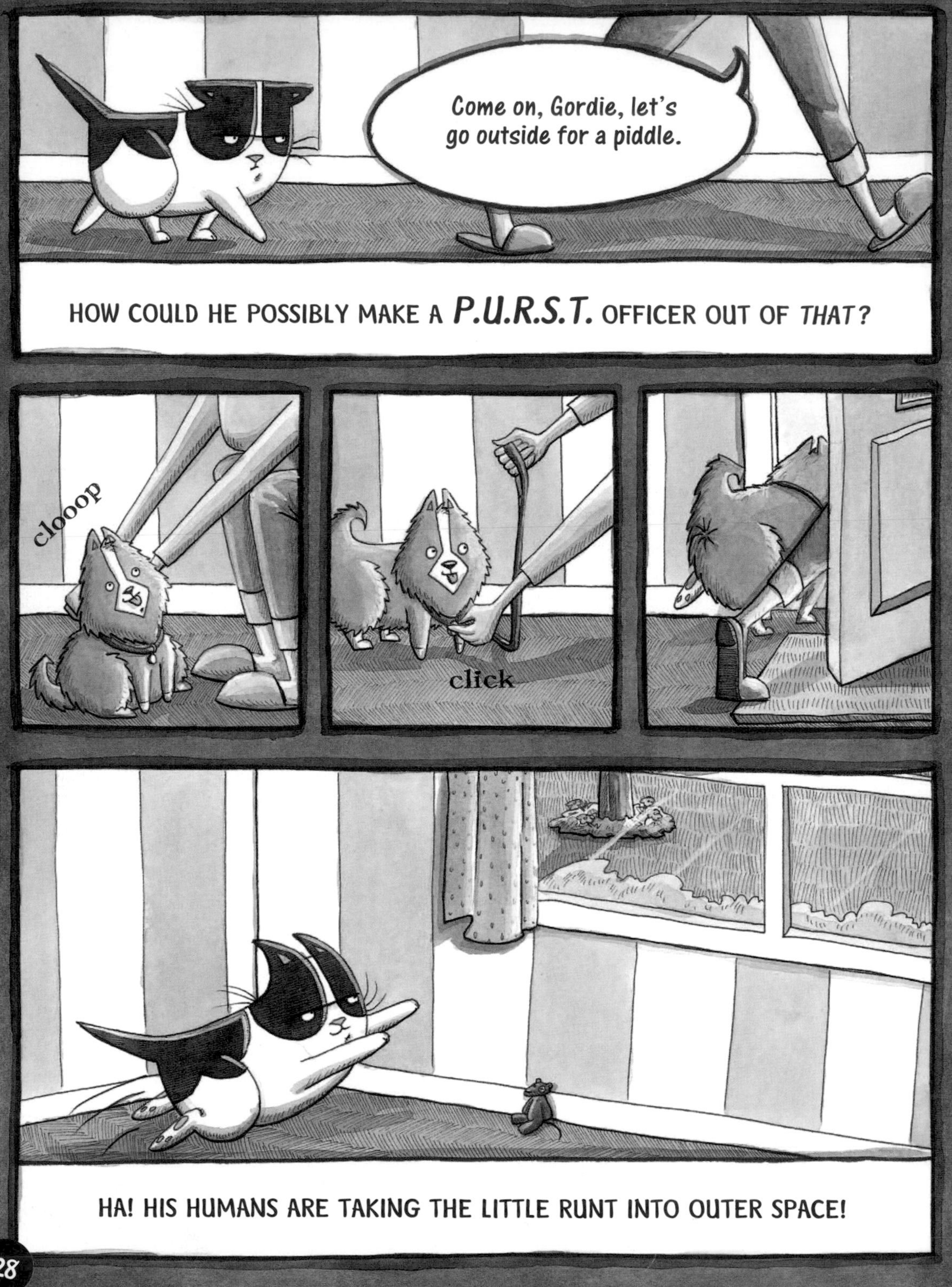
Come on, Gordie, let's go outside for a piddle.
HOW COULD HE POSSIBLY MAKE A P.U.R.S.T. OFFICER OUT OF THAT?
clooop
click
HA! HIS HUMANS ARE TAKING THE LITTLE RUNT INTO OUTER SPACE!

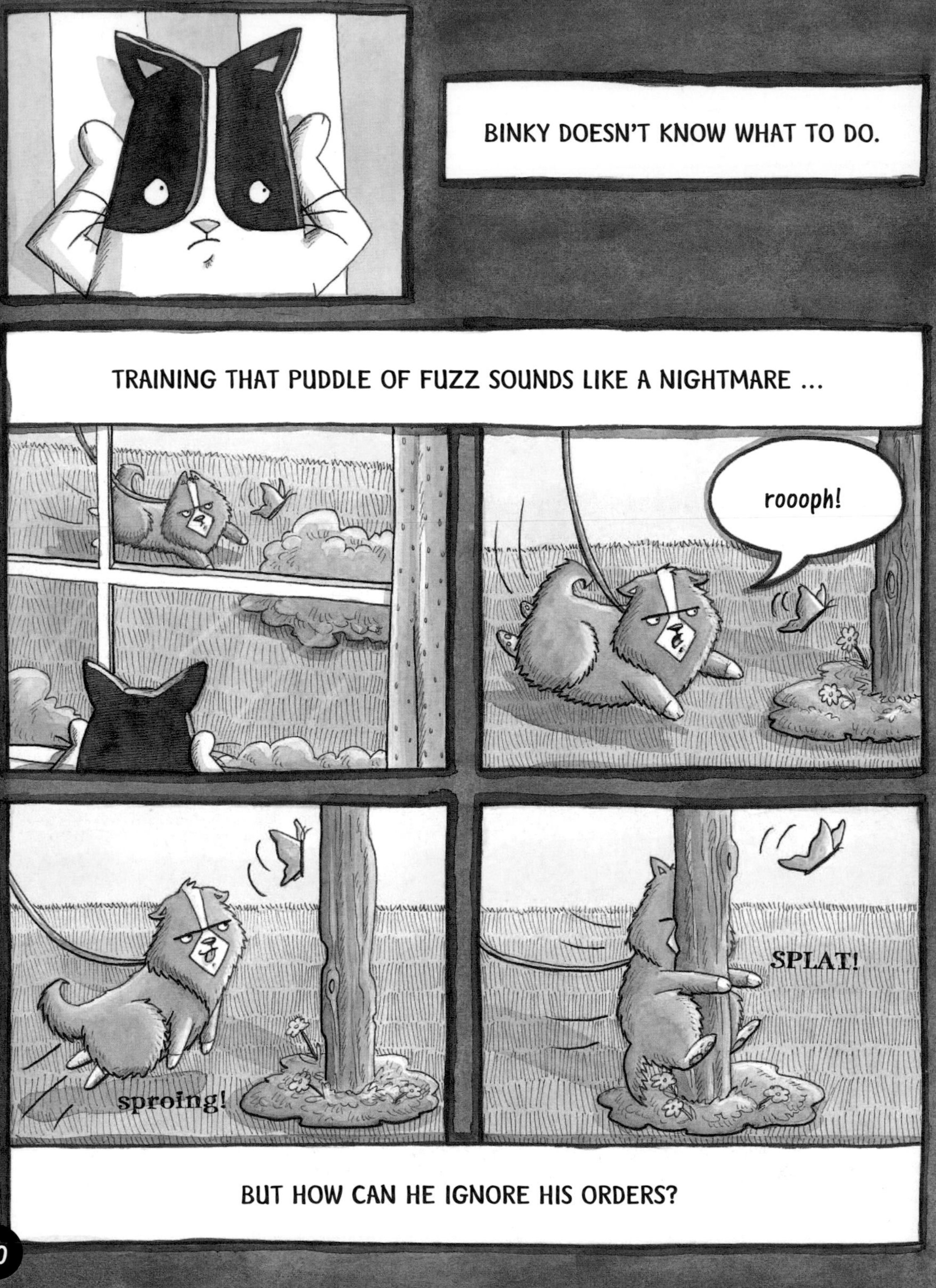
BINKY DOESN'T KNOW WHAT TO DO.
TRAINING THAT PUDDLE OF FUZZ SOUNDS LIKE A NIGHTMARE ...
roooph!
sproing!
SPLAT!
BUT HOW CAN HE IGNORE HIS ORDERS?

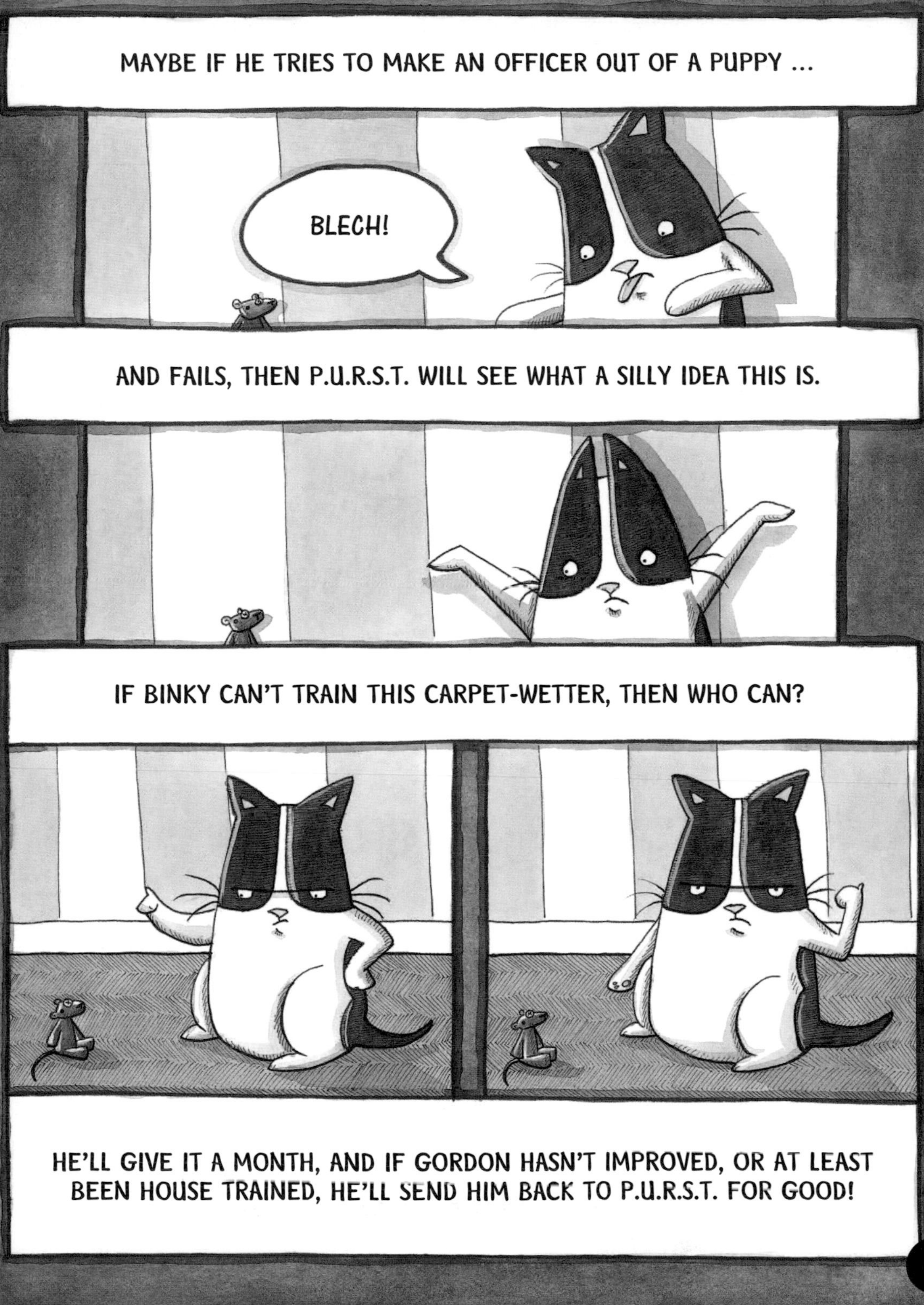

MAYBE IF HE TRIES TO MAKE AN OFFICER OUT OF A PUPPY ...
BLECH!
AND FAILS, THEN P.U.R.S.T. WILL SEE WHAT A SILLY IDEA THIS IS.
IF BINKY CAN'T TRAIN THIS CARPET-WETTER, THEN WHO CAN?
HE'LL GIVE IT A MONTH, AND IF GORDON HASN'T IMPROVED, OR AT LEAST BEEN HOUSE TRAINED, HE'LL SEND HIM BACK TO P.U.R.S.T. FOR GOOD!

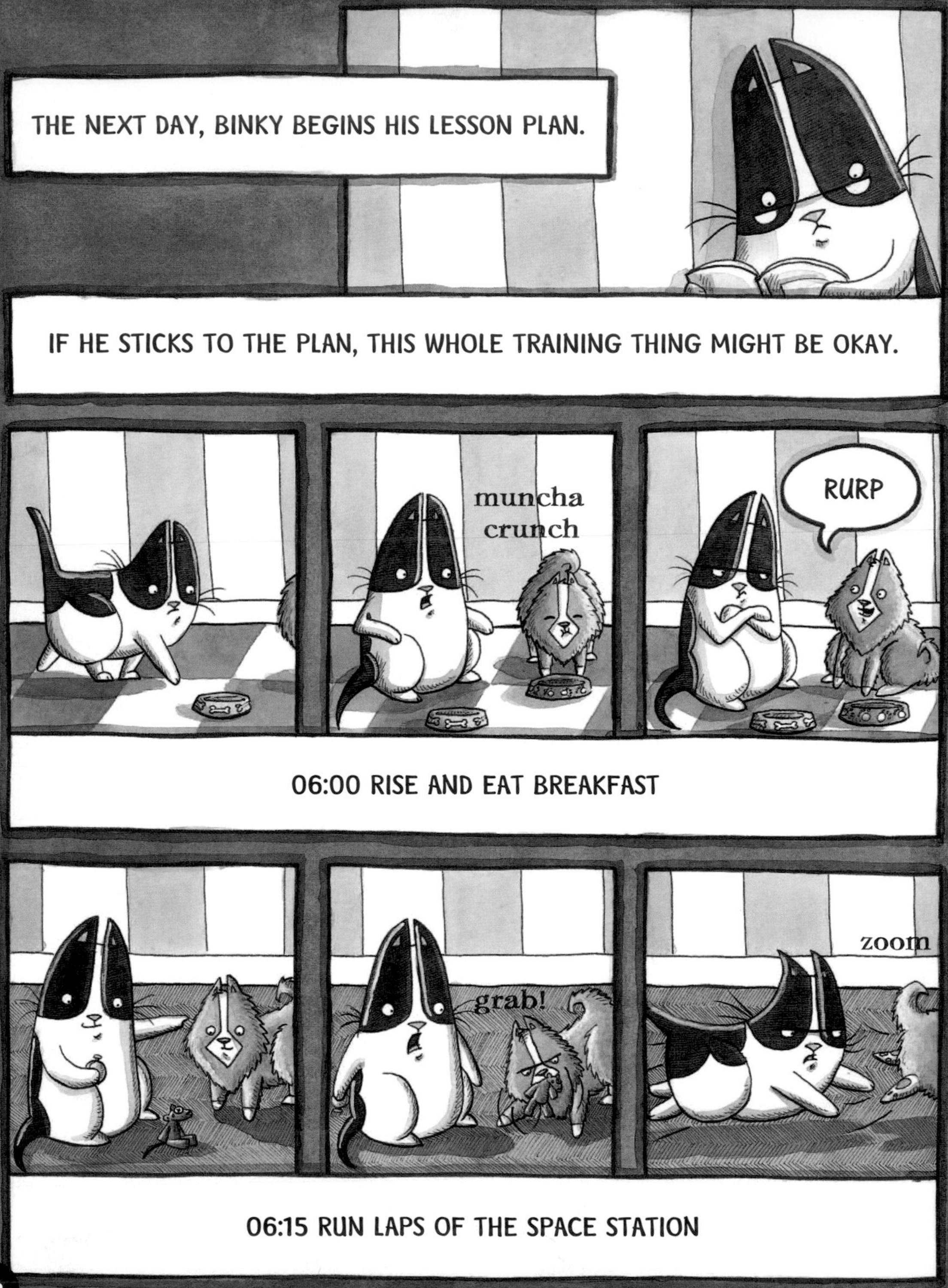
THE NEXT DAY, BINKY BEGINS HIS LESSON PLAN.
IF HE STICKS TO THE PLAN, THIS WHOLE TRAINING THING MIGHT BE OKAY.
muncha
crunch
RURP
06:00 RISE AND EAT BREAKFAST
grab!
zoom
06:15 RUN LAPS OF THE SPACE STATION

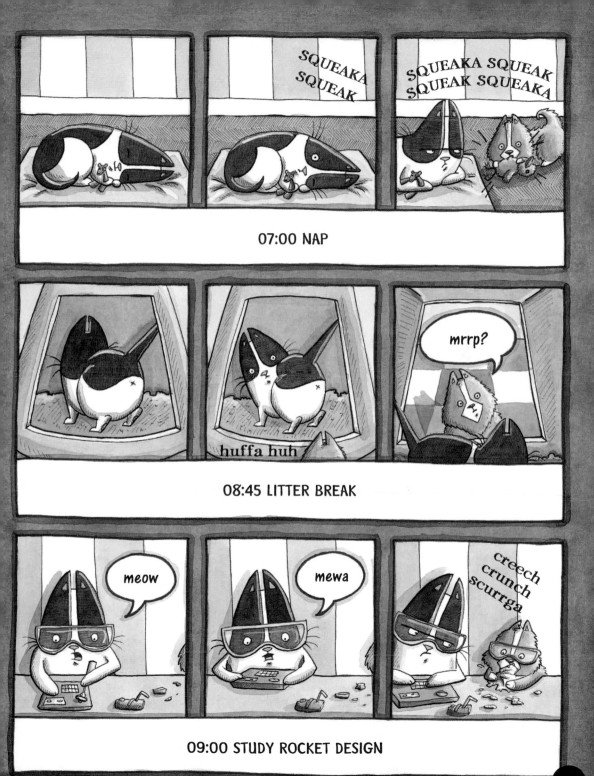

07:00 NAP

08:45 LITTER BREAK

09:00 STUDY ROCKET DESIGN

33

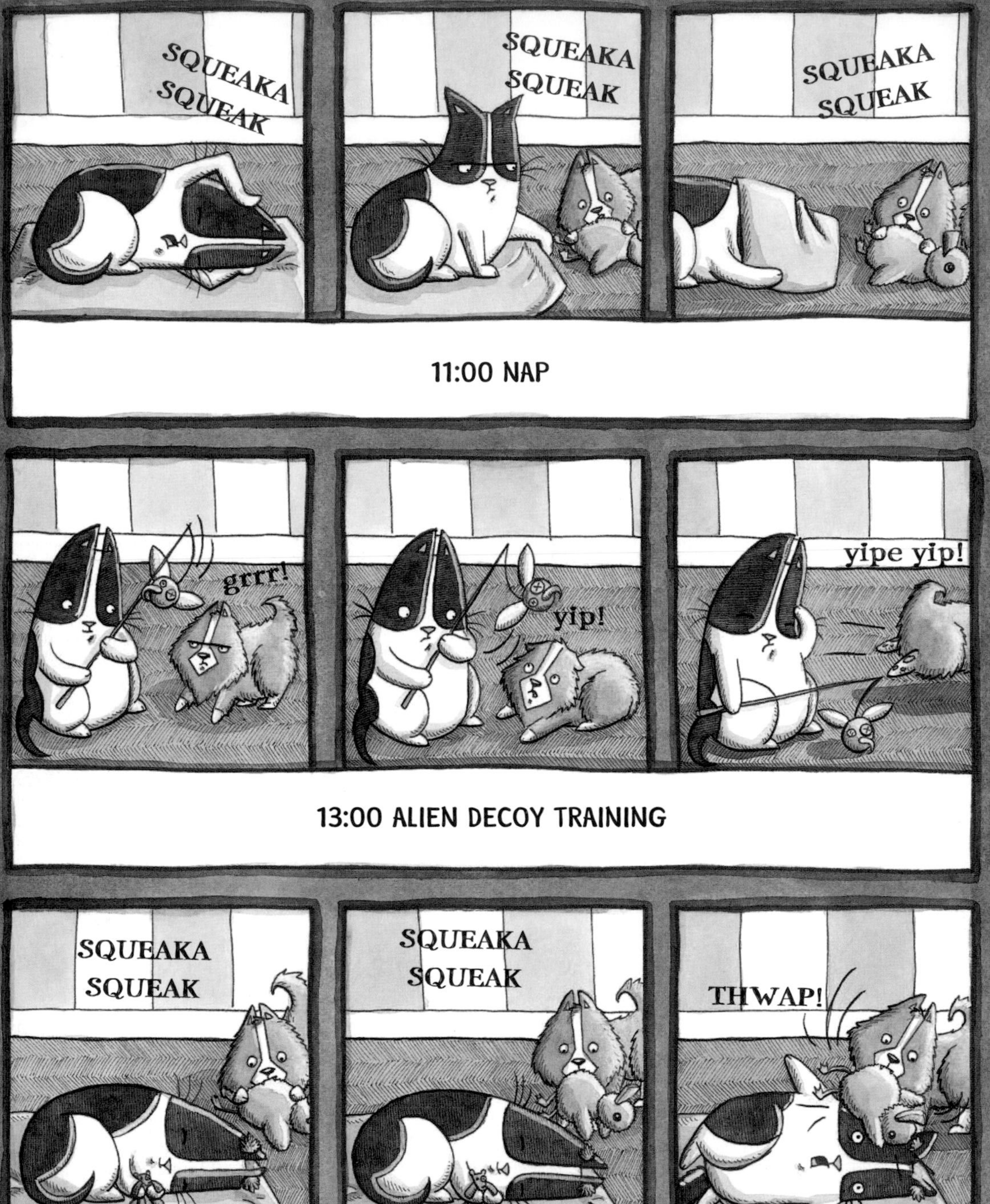
SQUEAKA SQUEAK
SQUEAKA SQUEAK
SQUEAKA SQUEAK
11:00 NAP
grrr!
yip!
yipe yip!
13:00 ALIEN DECOY TRAINING
SQUEAKA SQUEAK
SQUEAKA SQUEAK
THWAP!
15:00 NAP

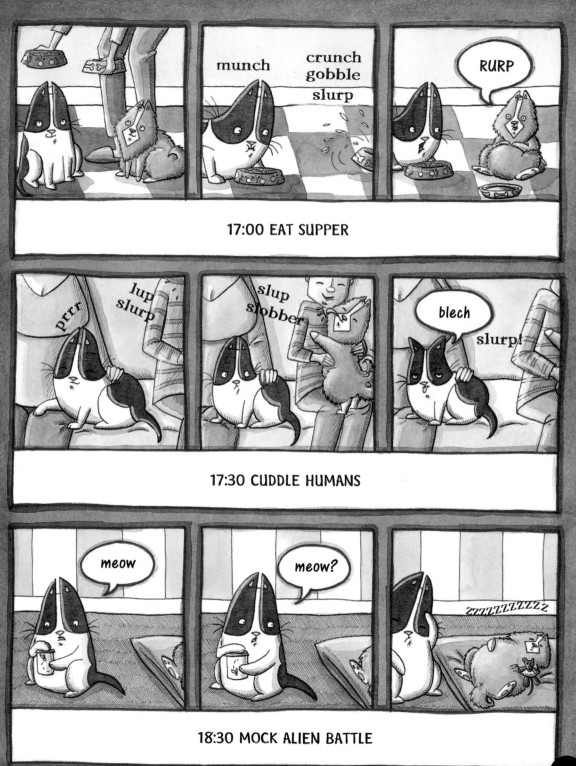

17:00 EAT SUPPER

17:30 CUDDLE HUMANS

18:30 MOCK ALIEN BATTLE

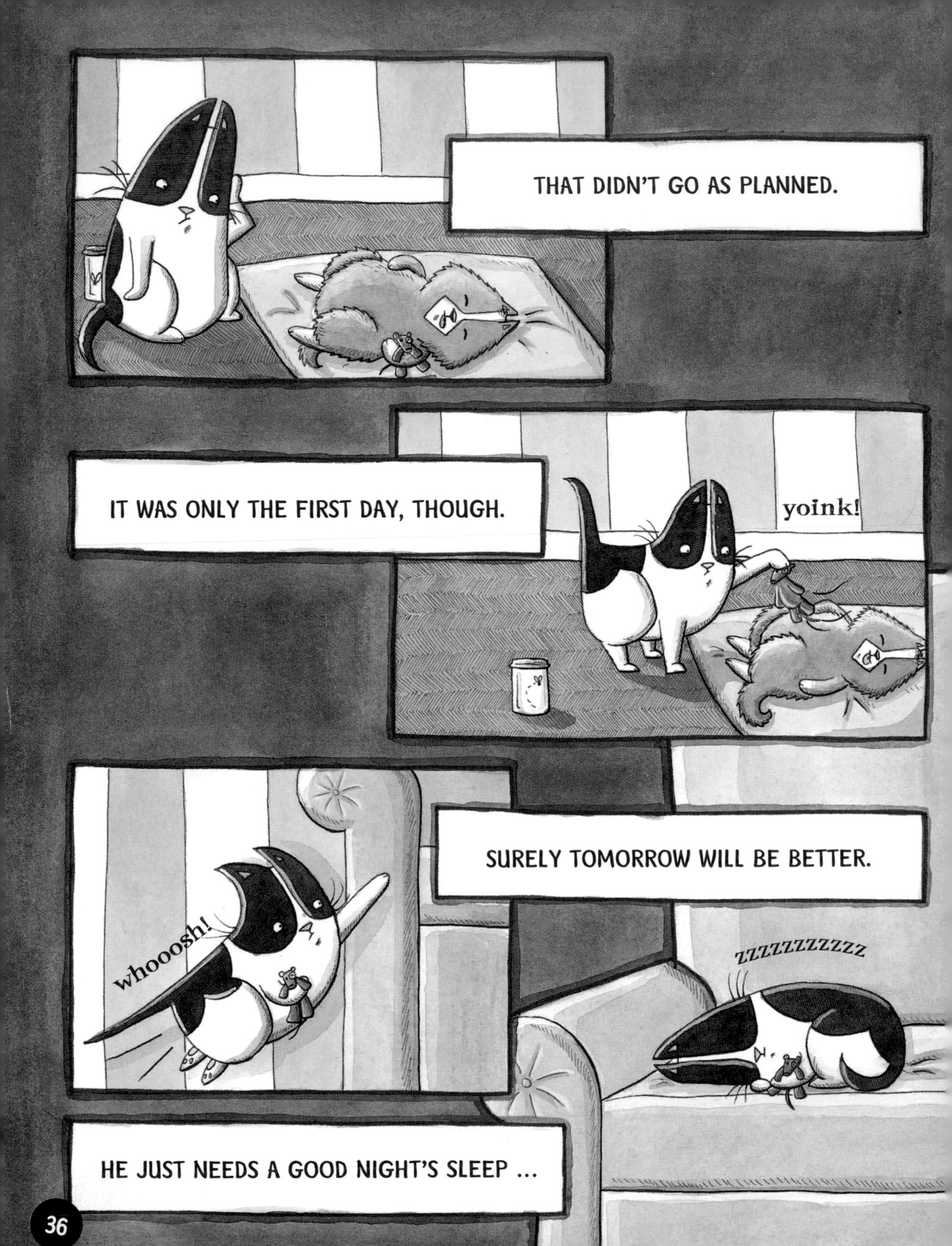
THAT DIDN'T GO AS PLANNED.
IT WAS ONLY THE FIRST DAY, THOUGH.
yoink!
SURELY TOMORROW WILL BE BETTER.
whooosh!
ZZZZZZZZZZZ
HE JUST NEEDS A GOOD NIGHT'S SLEEP ...

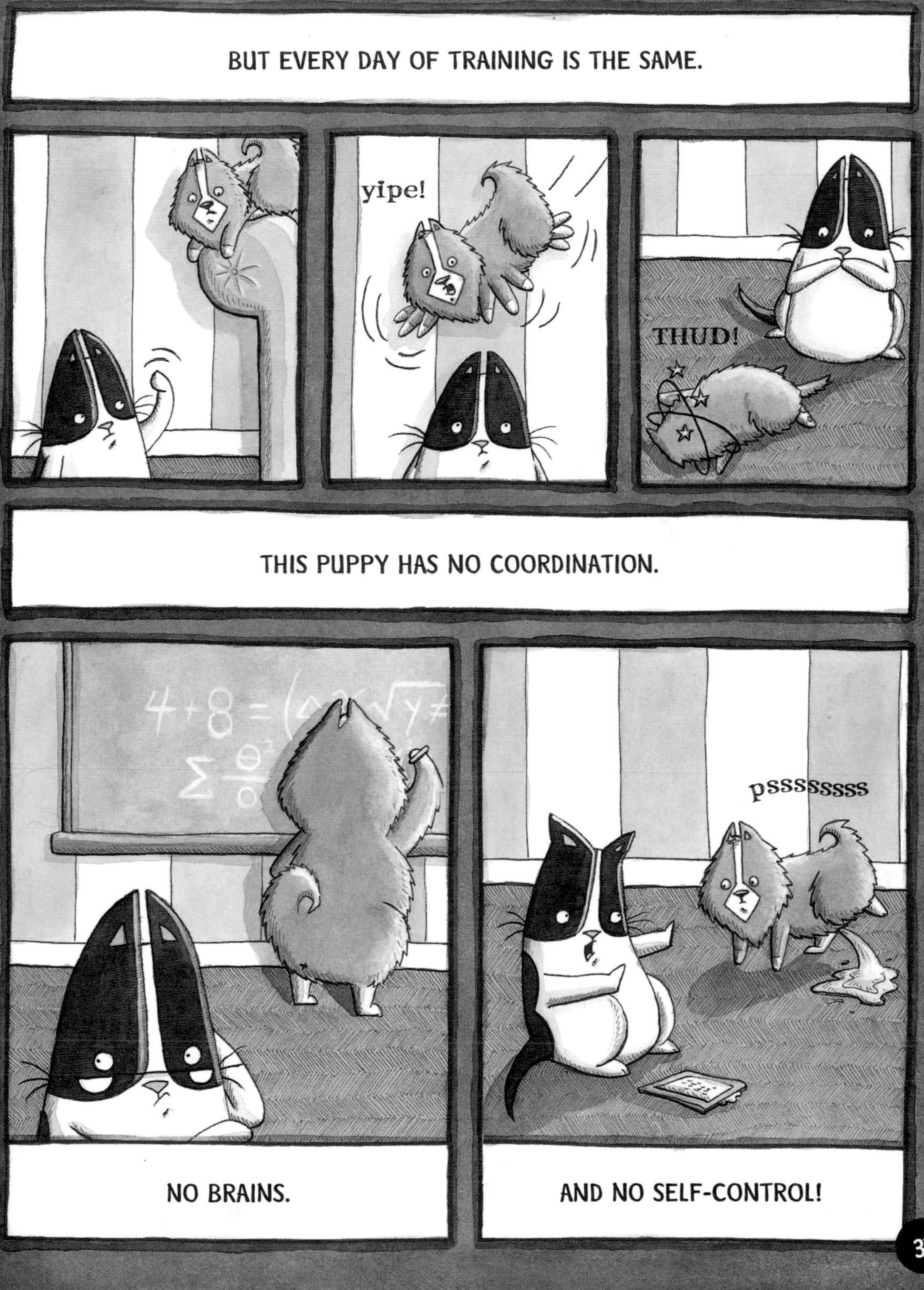
BUT EVERY DAY OF TRAINING IS THE SAME.
yipe!
THUD!
THIS PUPPY HAS NO COORDINATION.
NO BRAINS.
pssssssss
AND NO SELF-CONTROL!

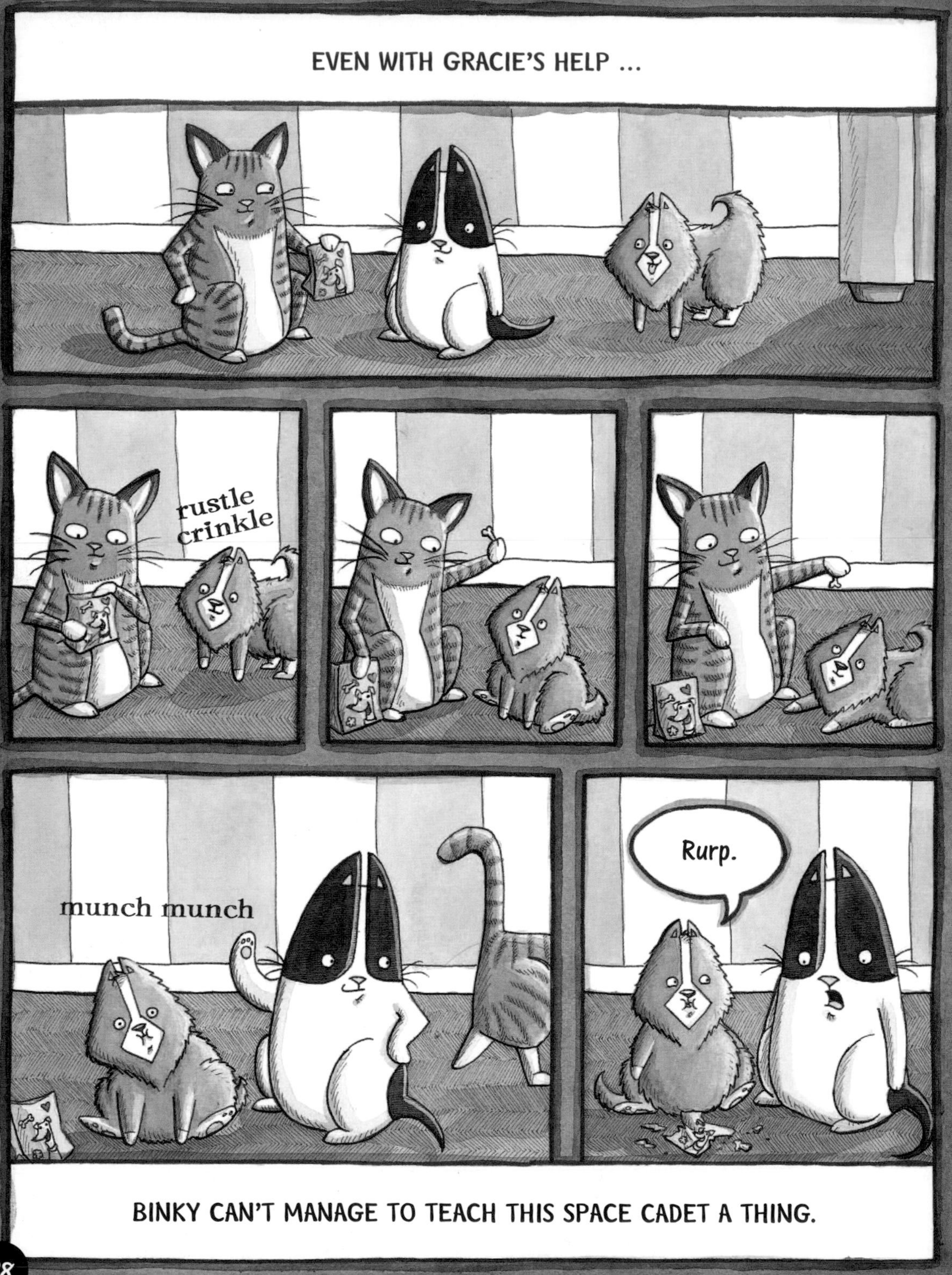
EVEN WITH GRACIE'S HELP ...
rustle
crinkle
munch munch
Rurp.
BINKY CAN'T MANAGE TO TEACH THIS SPACE CADET A THING.

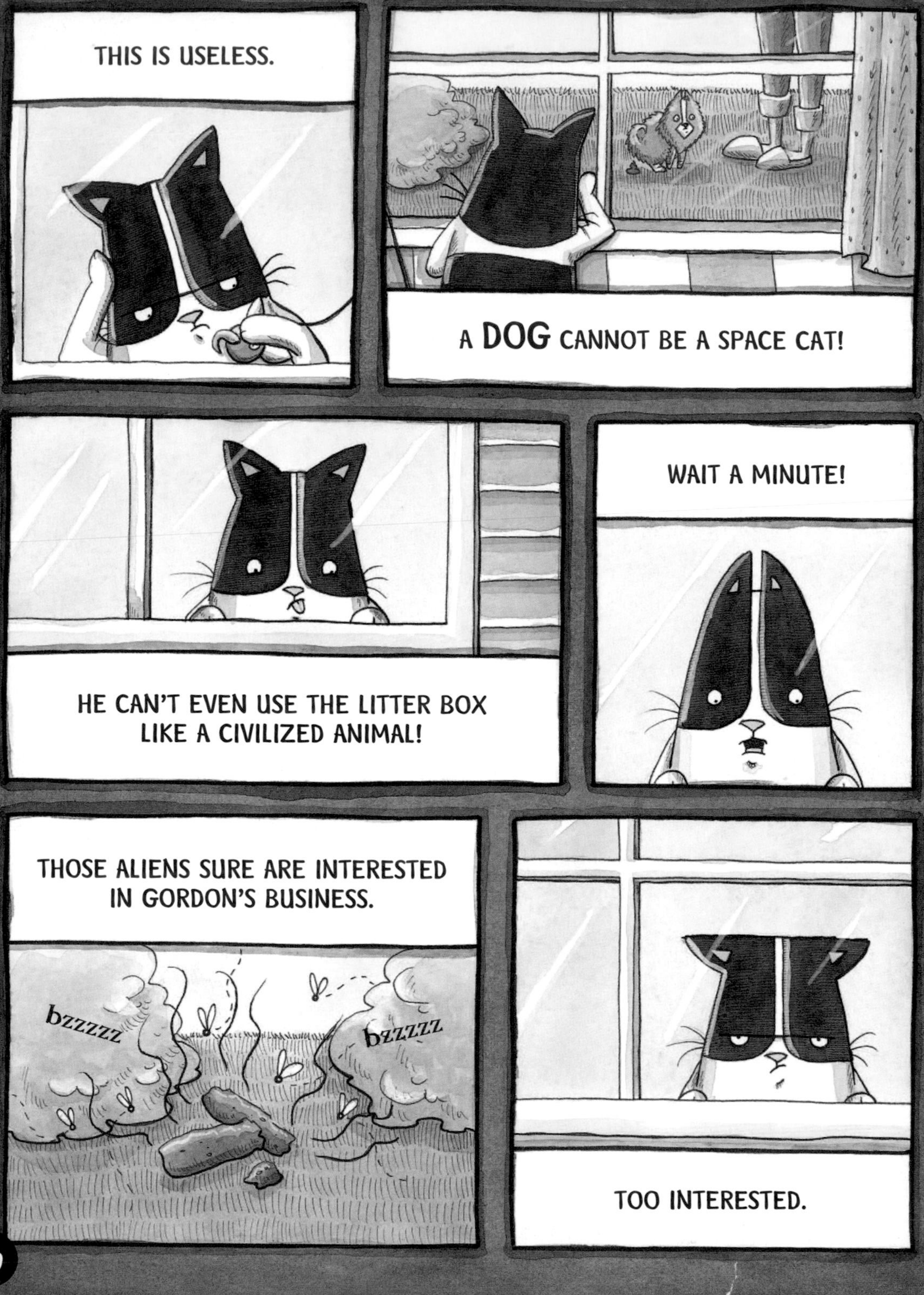

THIS IS USELESS.
A DOG CANNOT BE A SPACE CAT!
HE CAN'T EVEN USE THE LITTER BOX LIKE A CIVILIZED ANIMAL!
WAIT A MINUTE!
THOSE ALIENS SURE ARE INTERESTED IN GORDON'S BUSINESS.
bzzzzz
bzzzzz
TOO INTERESTED.

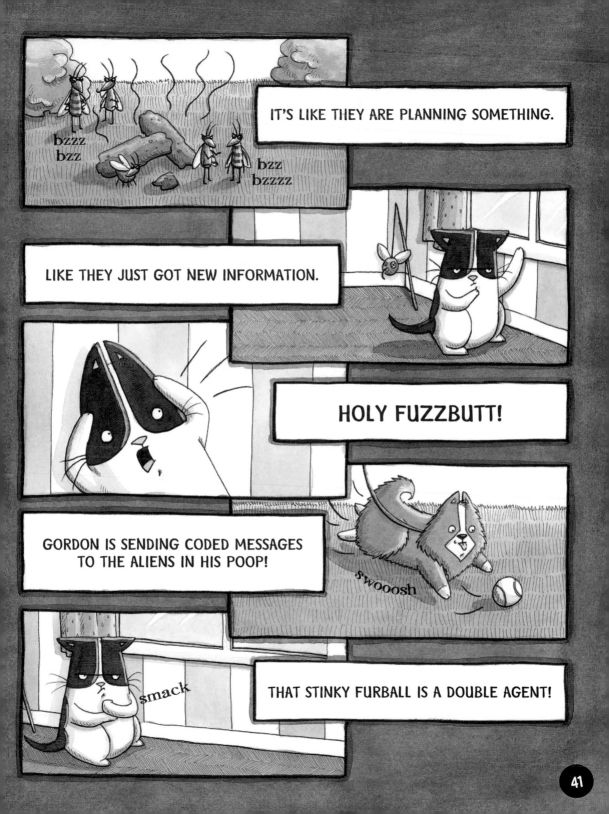

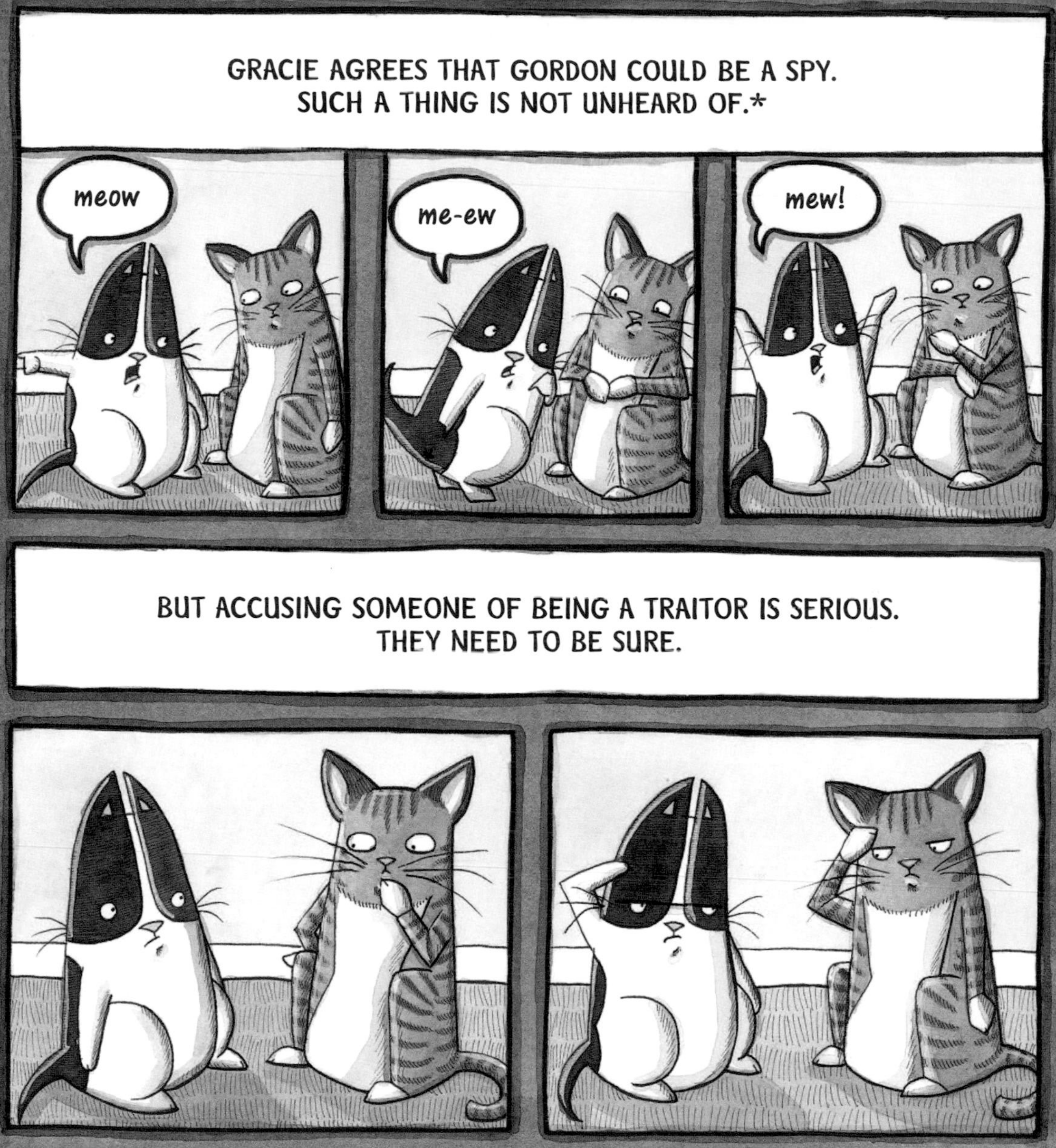
GRACIE AGREES THAT GORDON COULD BE A SPY.
SUCH A THING IS NOT UNHEARD OF.*
meow
me-ew
mew!
BUT ACCUSING SOMEONE OF BEING A TRAITOR IS SERIOUS.
THEY NEED TO BE SURE.

*THERE IS A FAMOUS CASE OF A BRILLIANT SPACE CAT WHO SIDED WITH THE ALIENS. SHE WENT AWOL AND NO ONE HAS HEARD FROM HER SINCE. BUT THAT'S ANOTHER STORY ...

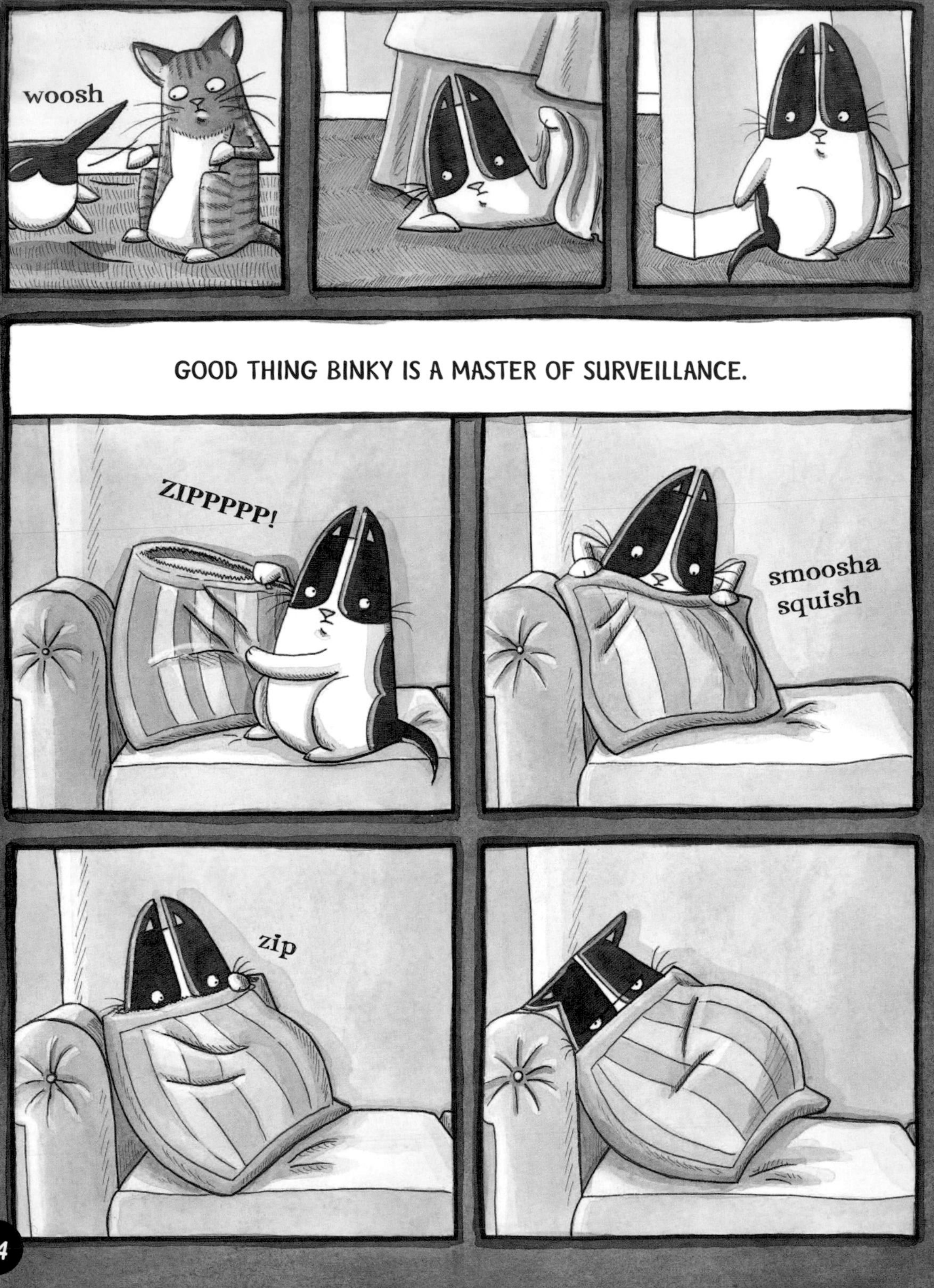
woosh
GOOD THING BINKY IS A MASTER OF SURVEILLANCE.
ZIPPPPP!
smoosha
squish
zip

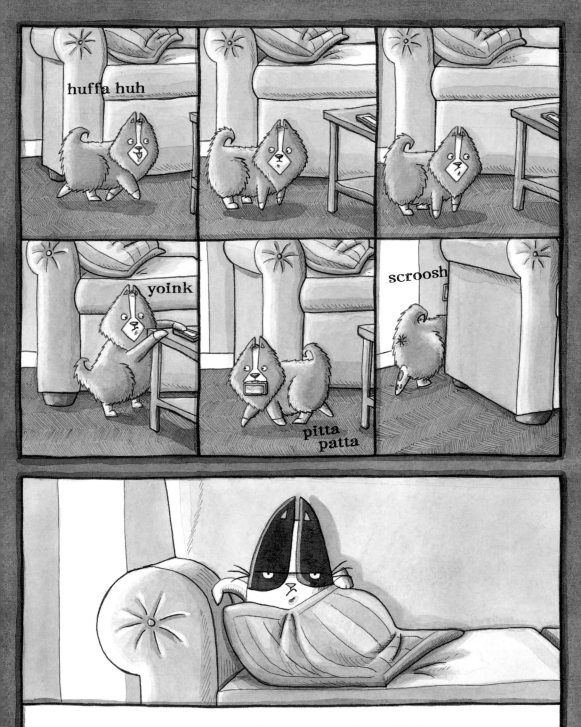

THE LITTLE RUNT IS A SPY AND A THIEF!

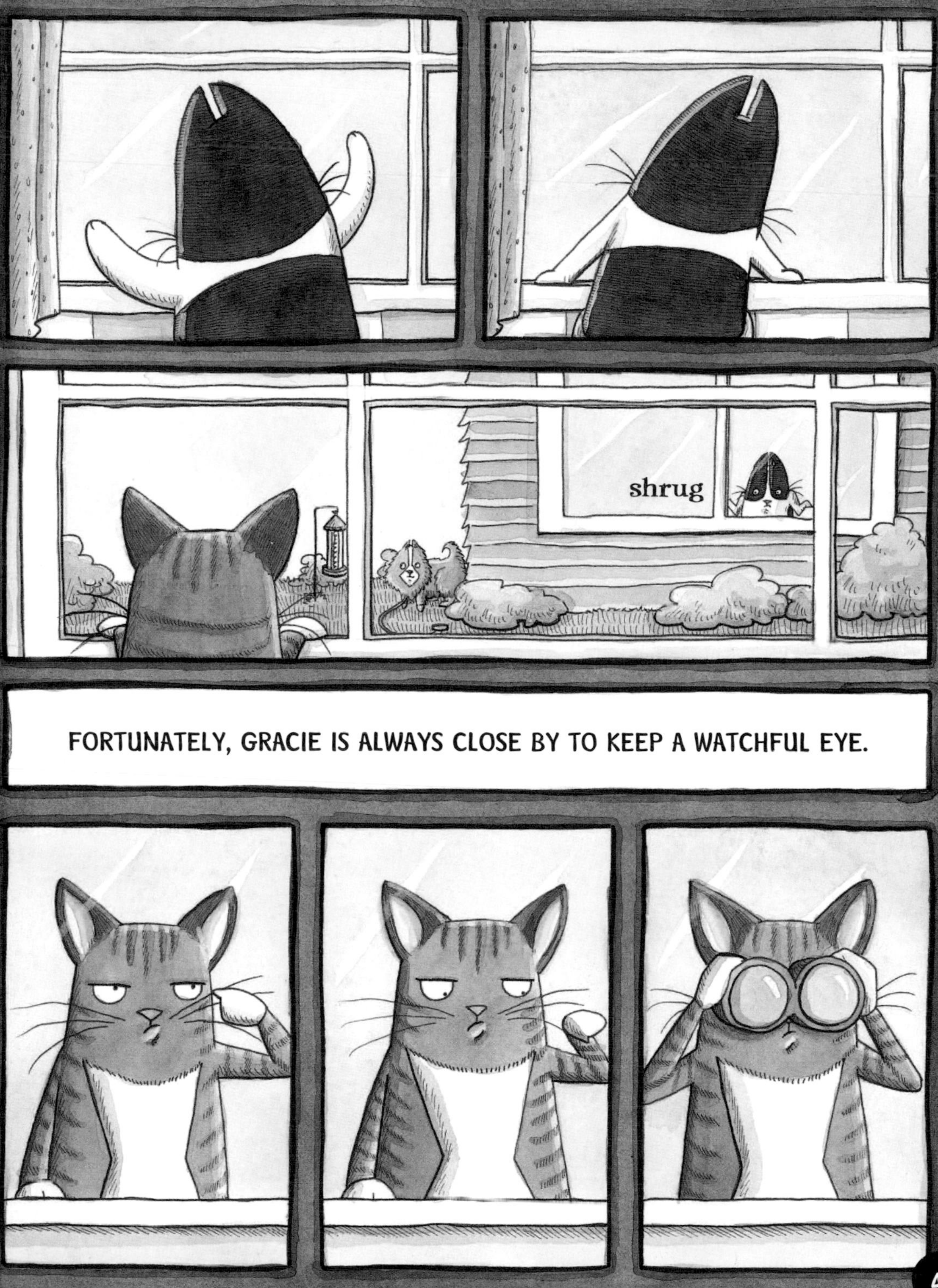
shrug
FORTUNATELY, GRACIE IS ALWAYS CLOSE BY TO KEEP A WATCHFUL EYE.

WHAT IS GORDON DOING WITH THAT ANTI-ALIEN DEVICE?

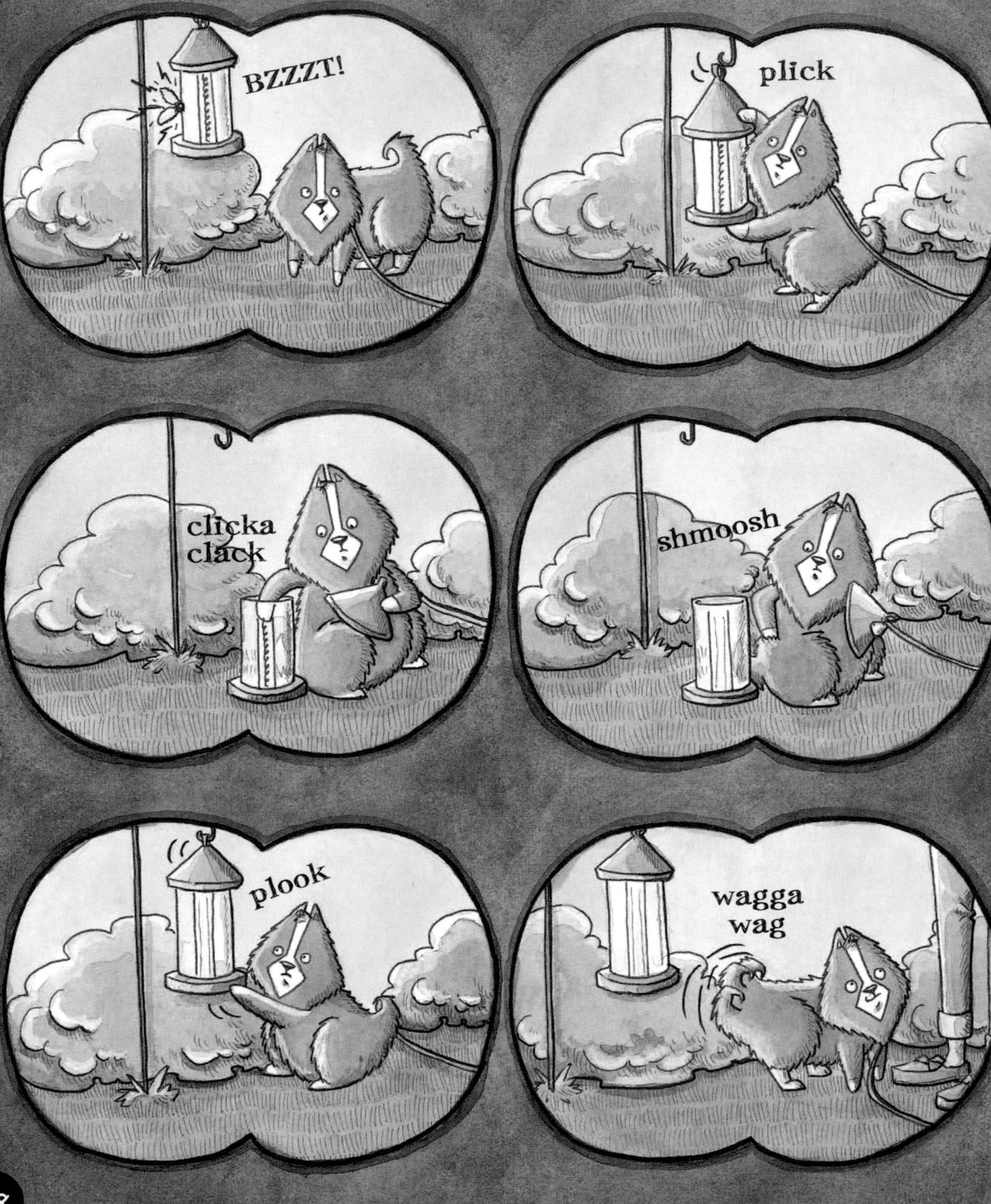
BZZZT!
plick
clicka clack
shmoosh
plook
wagga wag

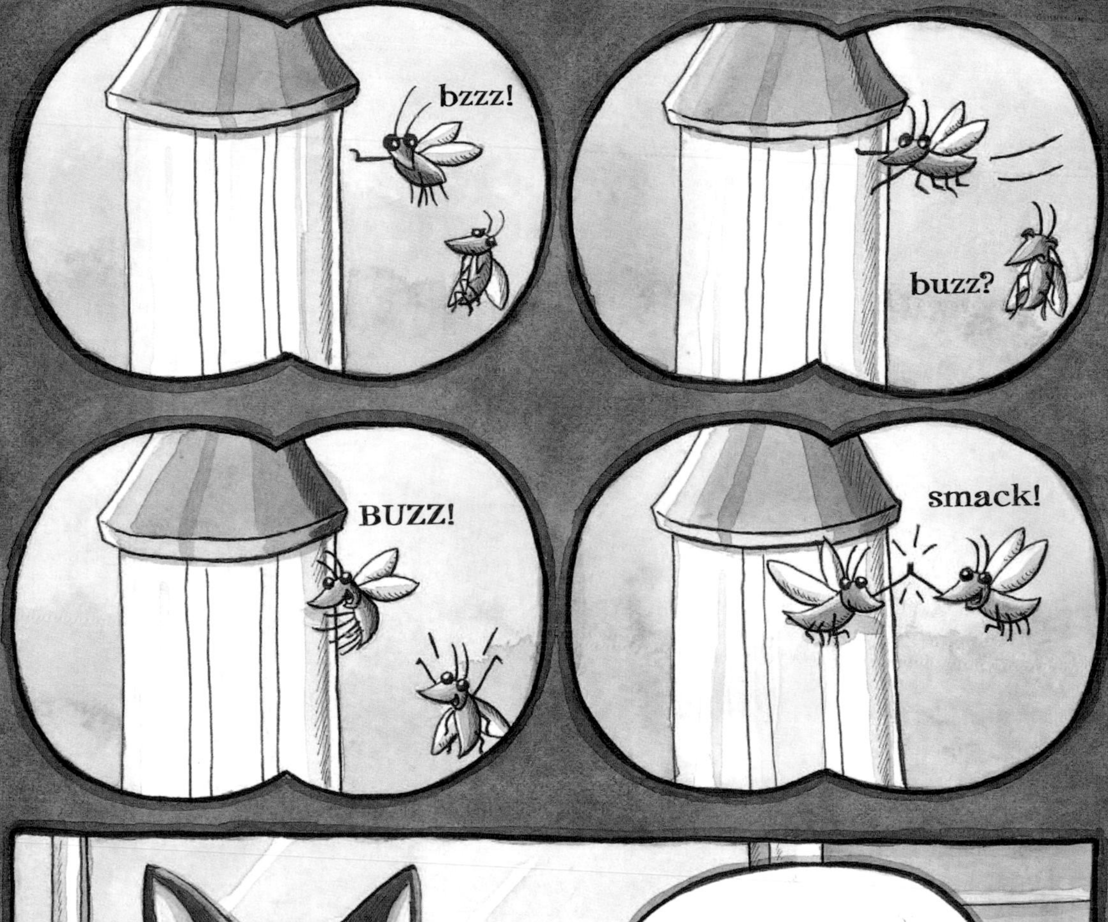
bzzz!
buzz?
BUZZ!
smack!
GASP!
HE DISARMED IT!

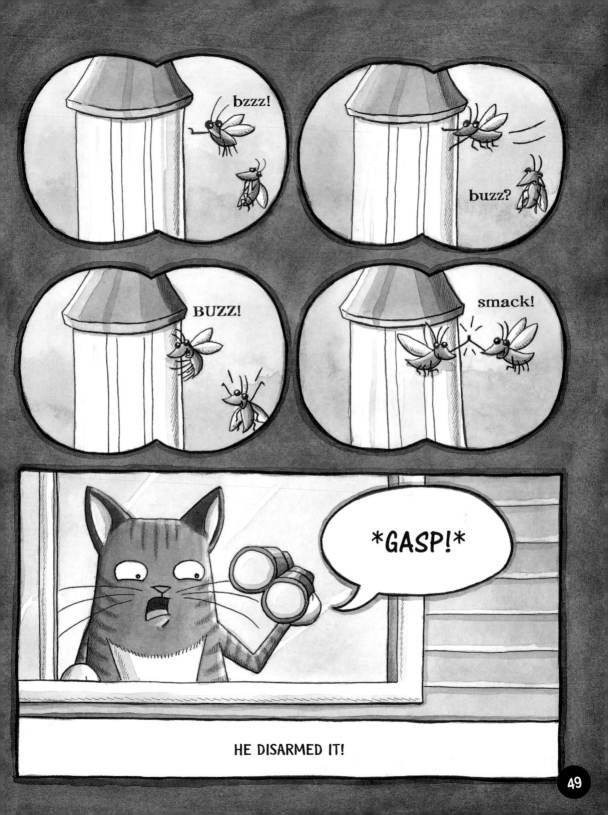

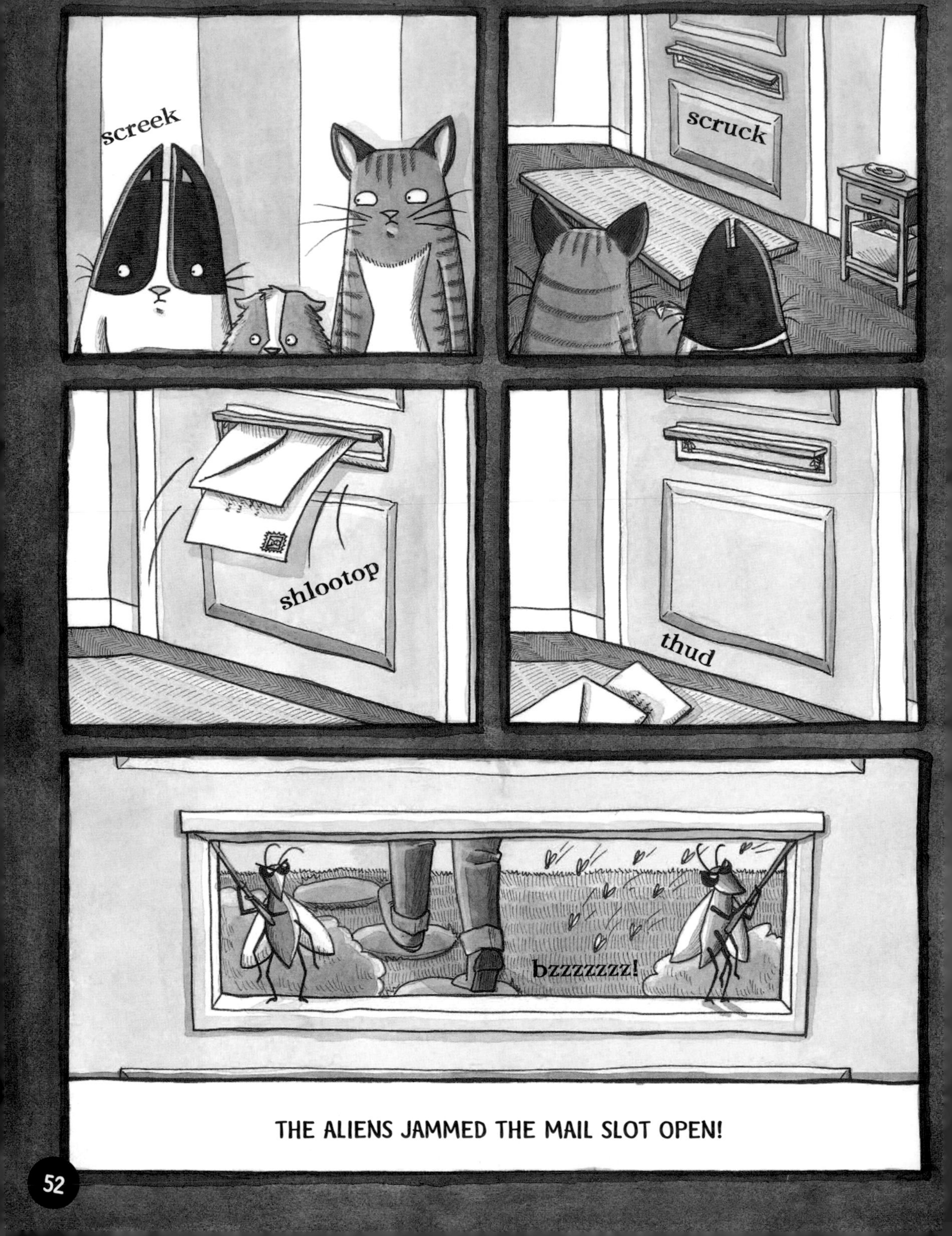
screek
scruck
shlootop
thud
bzzzzzzz!
THE ALIENS JAMMED THE MAIL SLOT OPEN!

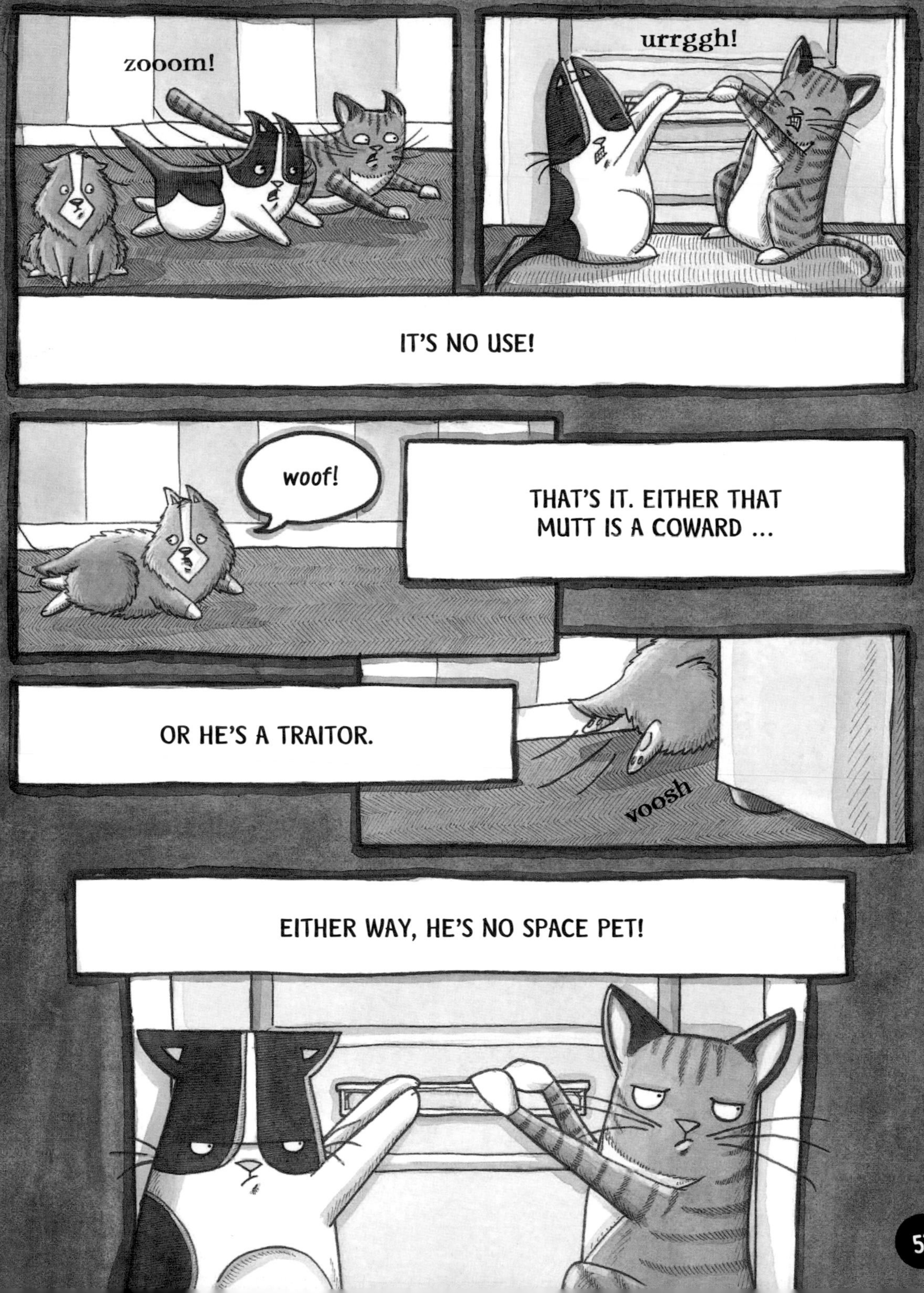

zooom!
urrggh!
IT'S NO USE!
woof!
THAT'S IT. EITHER THAT MUTT IS A COWARD ...
OR HE'S A TRAITOR.
voosh
EITHER WAY, HE'S NO SPACE PET!

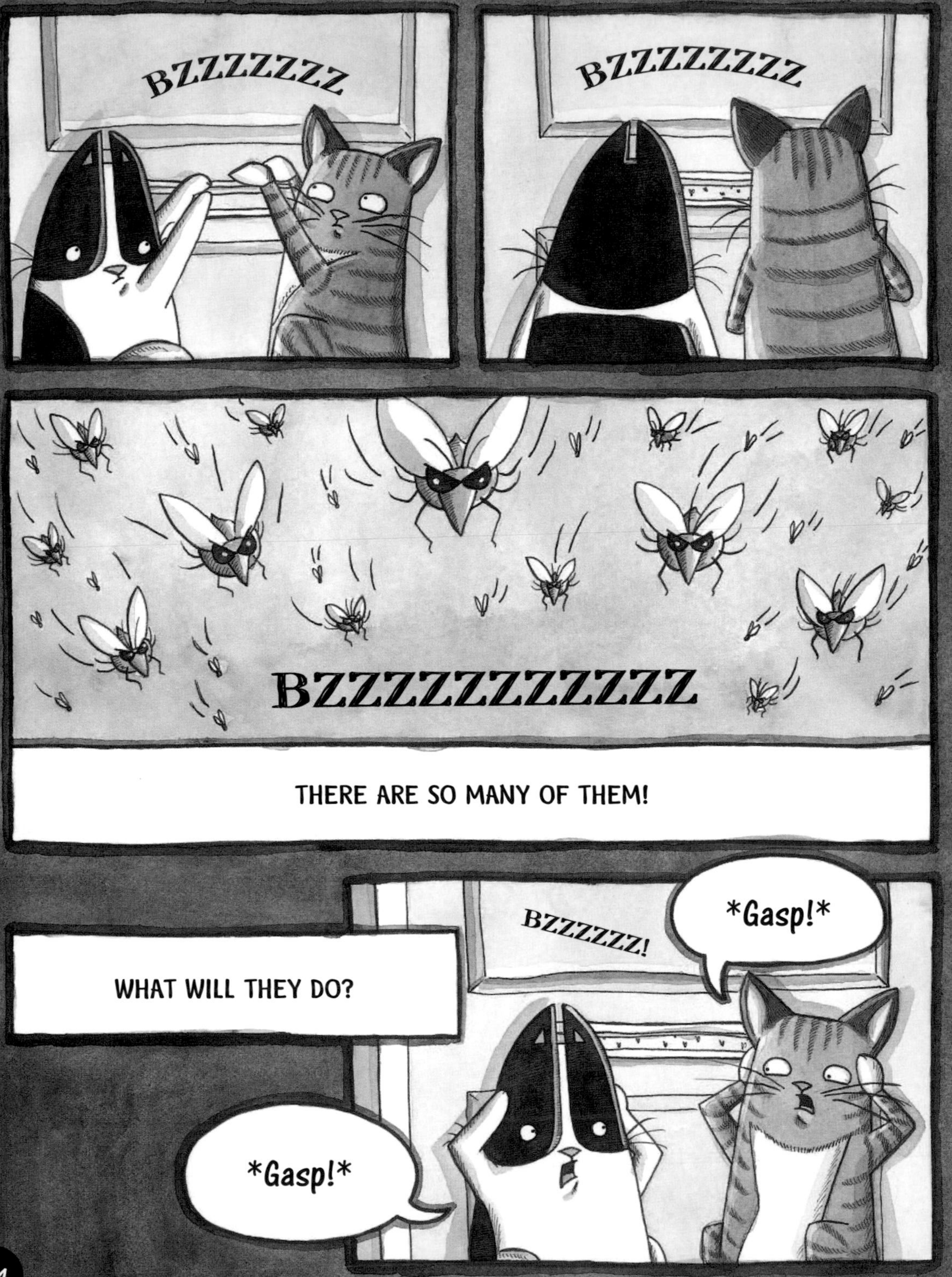
BZZZZZZZ
BZZZZZZZZ
BZZZZZZZZZZZZ
THERE ARE SO MANY OF THEM!
WHAT WILL THEY DO?
BZZZZZZ!
Gasp!
Gasp!

55

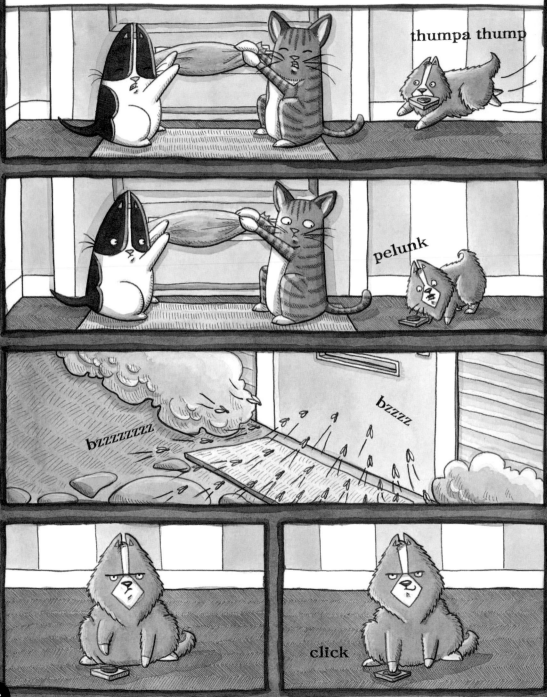

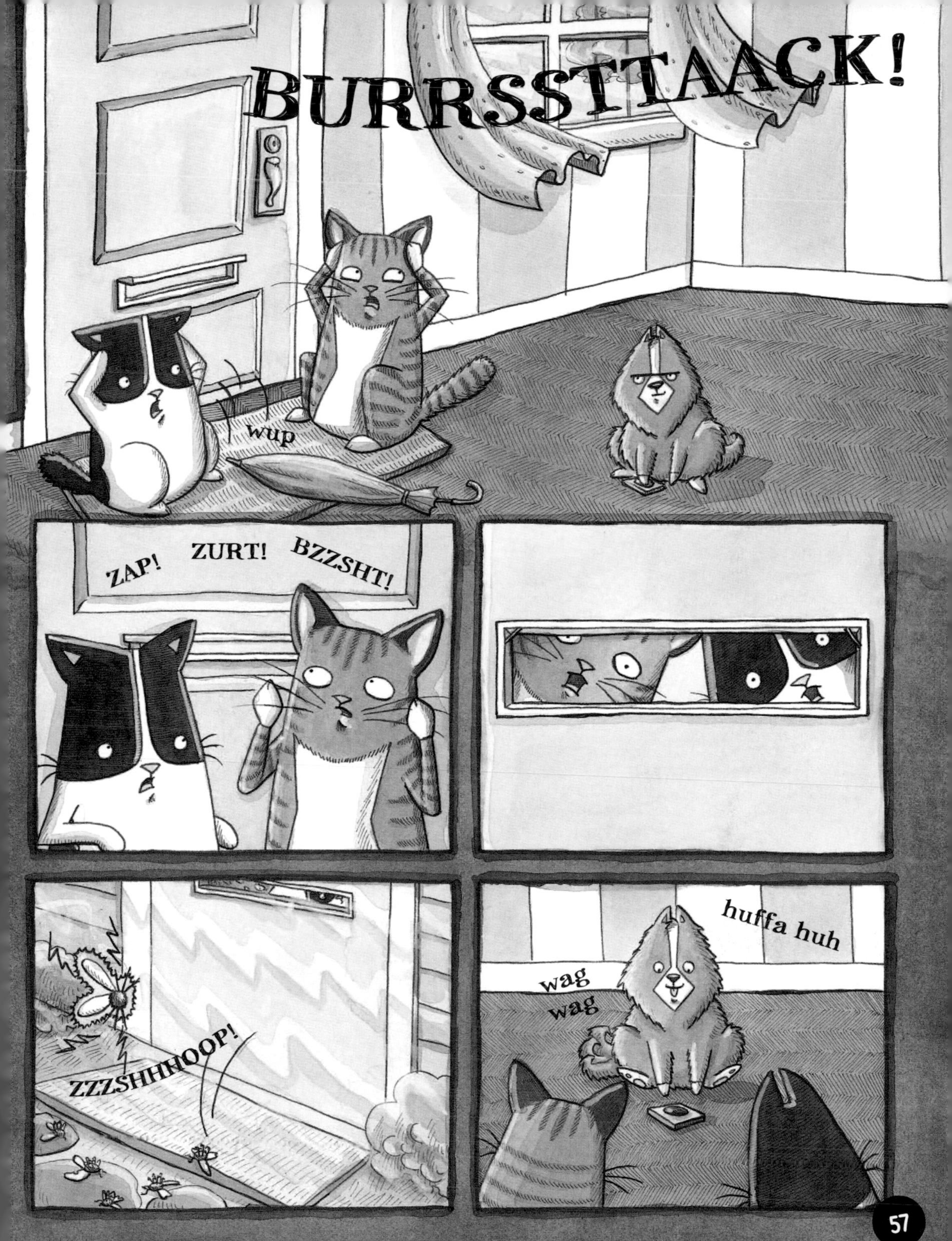
BURRSSTTAACK!
wup
ZAP!
ZURT!
BZZSHT!
ZZZSHHHOOP!
huffa huh
wag
wag

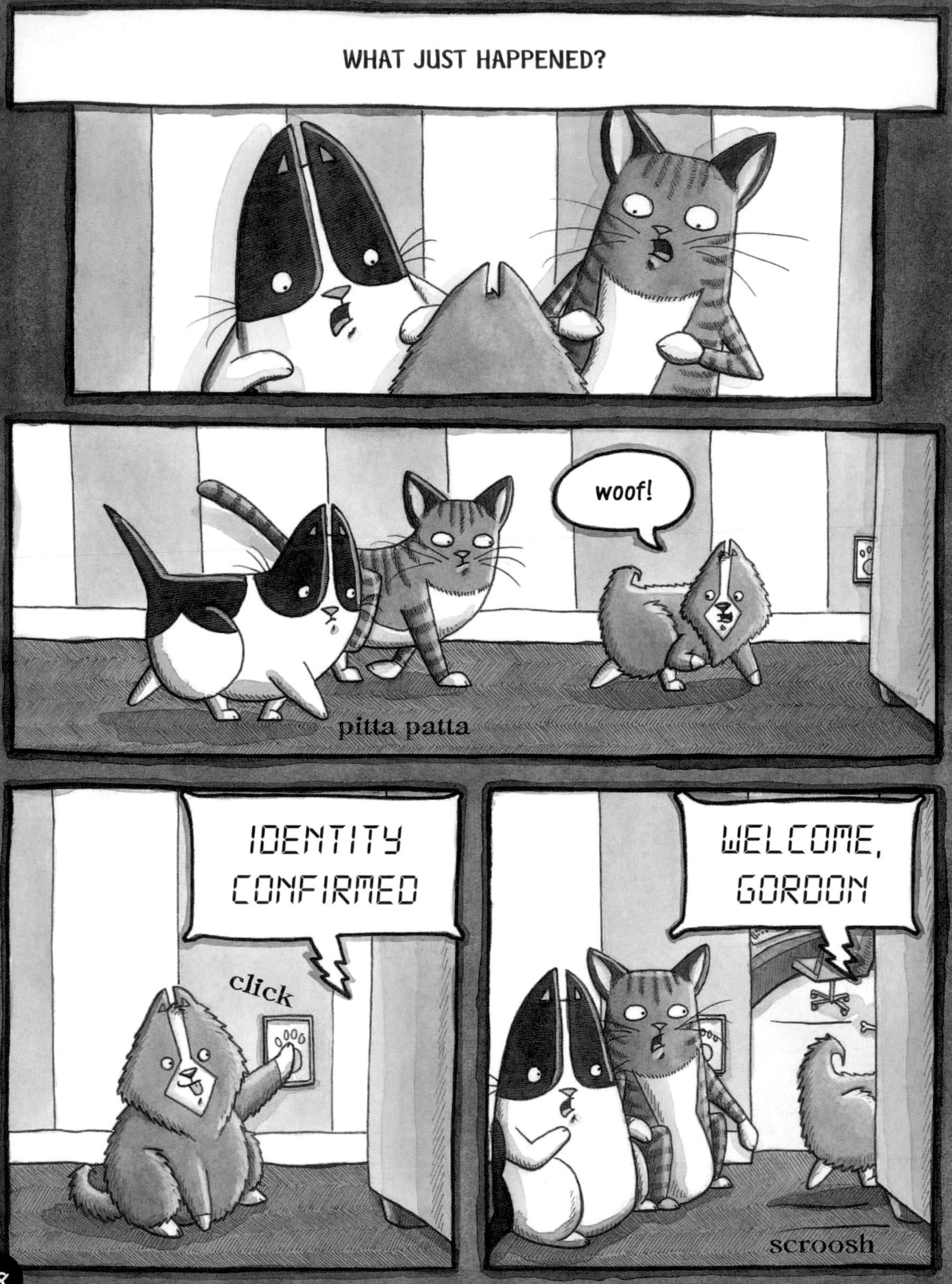
WHAT JUST HAPPENED?
woof!
pitta patta
IDENTITY CONFIRMED
click
WELCOME, GORDON
scroosh

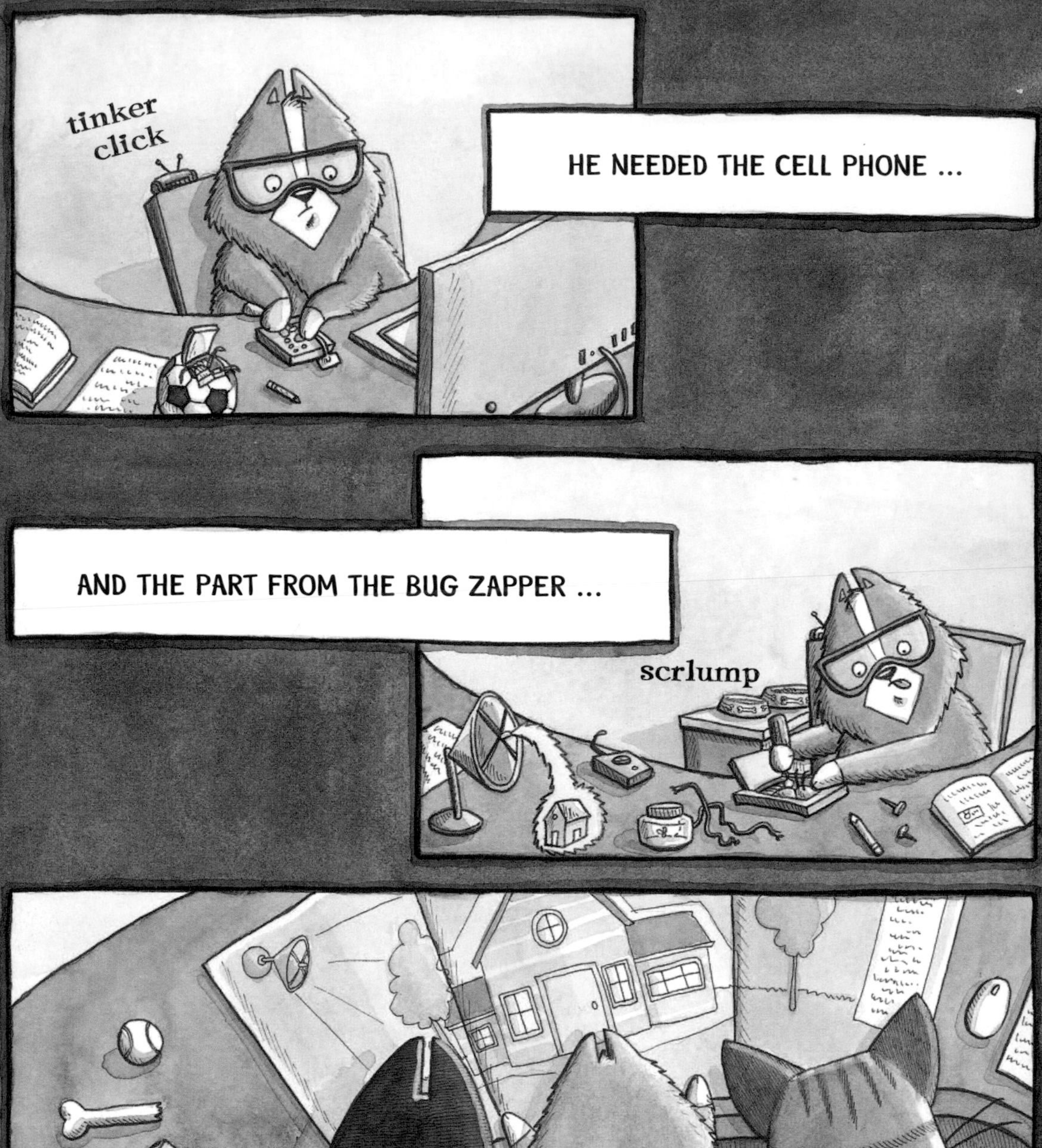
tinker
click
HE NEEDED THE CELL PHONE ...
AND THE PART FROM THE BUG ZAPPER ...
scrlump
TO CREATE AN ANTI-ALIEN FORCE FIELD THAT COVERS THE WHOLE BUILDING.

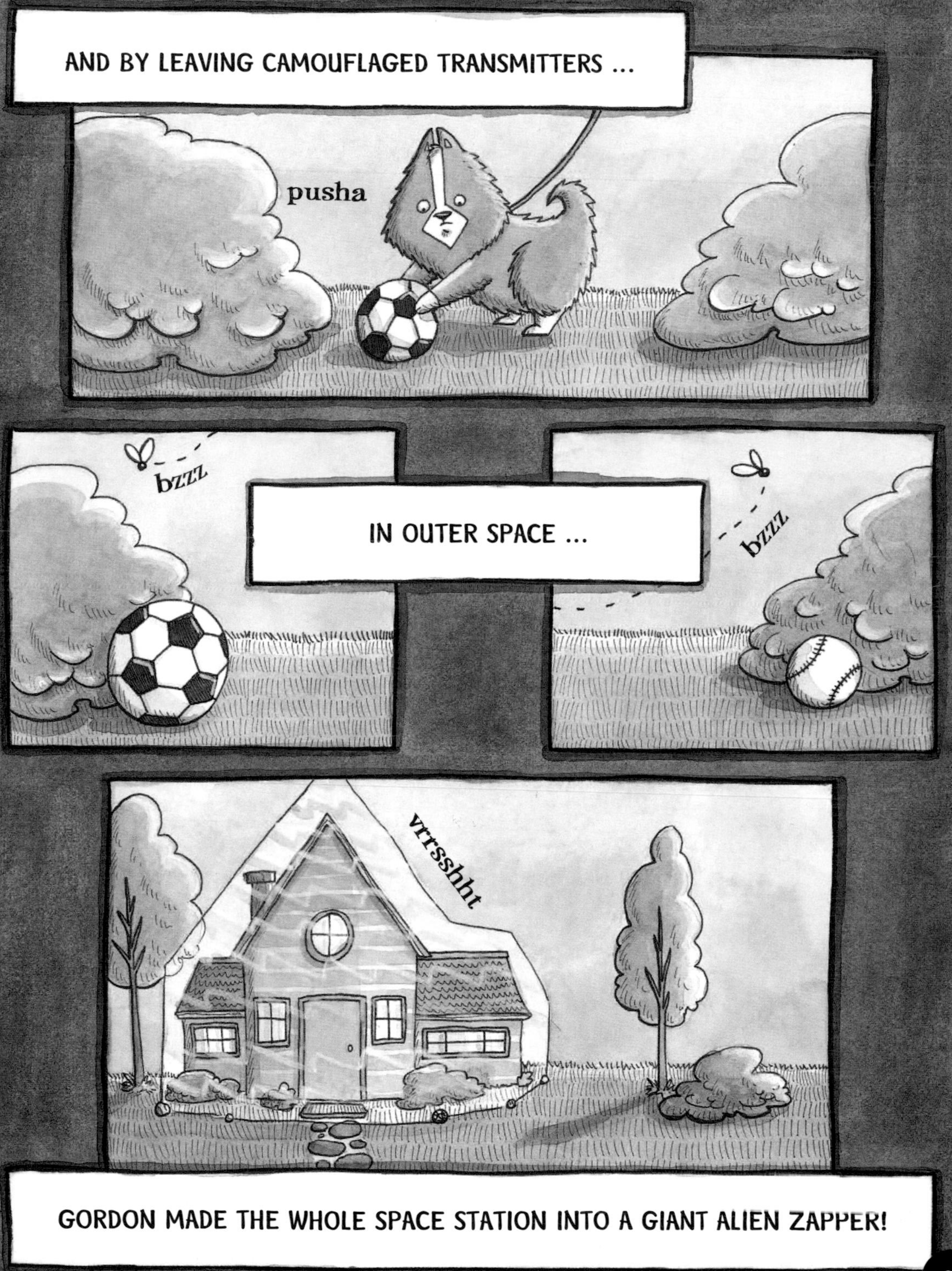
AND BY LEAVING CAMOUFLAGED TRANSMITTERS ...
pusha
bzzz
IN OUTER SPACE ...
bzzz
vrrsshht
GORDON MADE THE WHOLE SPACE STATION INTO A GIANT ALIEN ZAPPER!

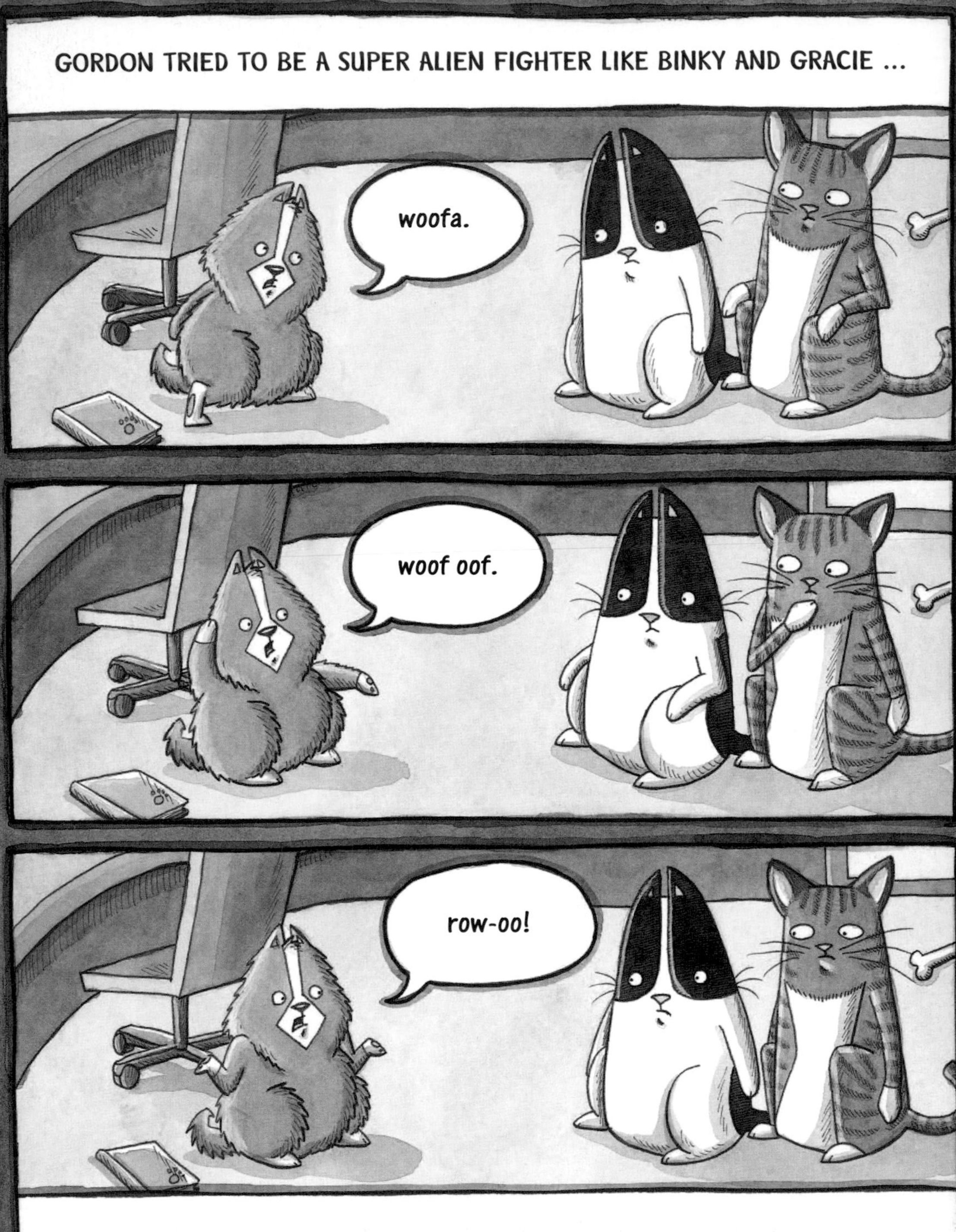
GORDON TRIED TO BE A SUPER ALIEN FIGHTER LIKE BINKY AND GRACIE ...
woofa.
woof oof.
row-oo!
BUT HE CAN'T LEAP OR POUNCE OR CLAW VERY WELL.

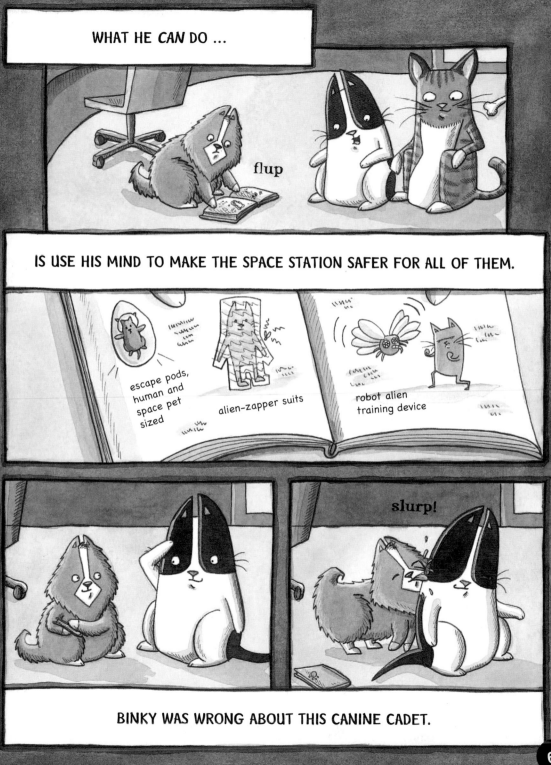

WHAT HE *CAN* DO ...

flup

IS USE HIS MIND TO MAKE THE SPACE STATION SAFER FOR ALL OF THEM.

escape pods, human and space pet sized

alien-zapper suits

robot alien training device

slurp!

BINKY WAS WRONG ABOUT THIS CANINE CADET.

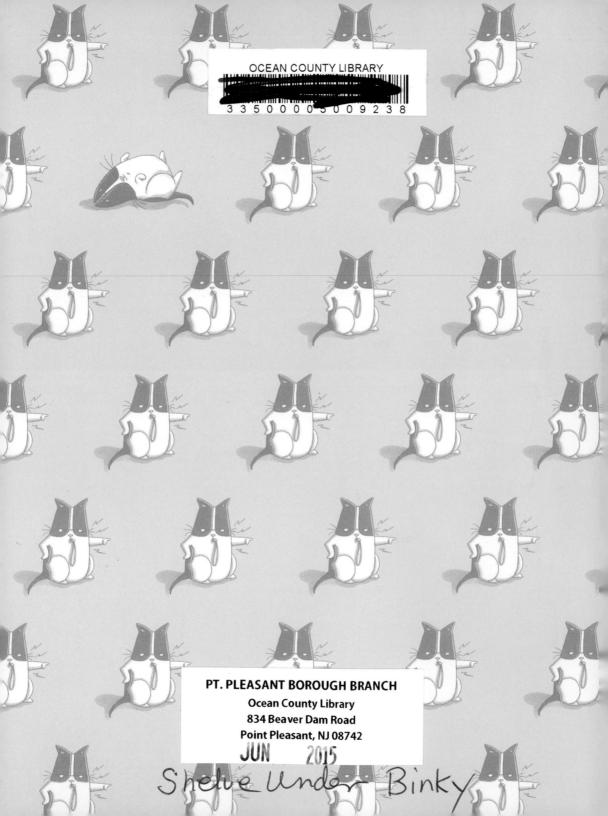

OCEAN COUNTY LIBRARY

3 3 5 0 0 0 0 5 0 0 9 2 3 8

PT. PLEASANT BOROUGH BRANCH

Ocean County Library
834 Beaver Dam Road
Point Pleasant, NJ 08742

JUN   2015

Shelve Under Binky